# The Misadventures of Poopsie O'Flannigan

## LUDO FRANK

ΦAP PUBLISHING

*For Mom*

# Contents

# To See the World



*JUNE 8, 2002*

Iapplied for the governess position only because the job description promised travel abroad. Graduation from the state university was long overdue, and wanderlust has been tugging at my heartstrings for the last two and a half years. With my nose to the grindstone and ever in the books, I failed to answer her pull. Now, free from said grindstone but with outstanding obligation to my purse strings, I found the most economical way for me to travel.

Embracing the most potent tool of globalization, the Internet, I entered a search for au pair employment. A governess position in Chicago! The advertisement sought a governess for two young girls, aged ten and two. I was intrigued by their wording, 'governess,' not au pair or nanny as one would expect in the parlance of our times. It's a very Victorian communique, and I couldn't help but be intrigued. Completing my studies in English Literature with an emphasis on the Victorian era, I contemplated the possibility this position may be kismet and found the idea pleasing. What's more, the writers of the job posting promised frequent foreign travel. I answered the advertisement with an email.

I did leave behind dear friends in Chicago when I departed college suddenly and unexpectedly after a spectacularly bad acid trip. Wistfully, I recall the day my friend Leia and I went to the Art Institute of Chicago and afterward, stayed a little too long in the city drinking at a bar. Being as it was a Sunday night, we feared the trains to the suburbs had stopped running and we wouldn't make it back to the college campus.

"Let's go to Yo Mama's," Leia suggested.

"Yo Mama!" I retorted.

"Fuck you, Boopsie. Yo Mama's is a coffee shop where I know we can rent space in the basement to sleep overnight."

Intrigued, and open for any adventure with Leia, I consented.

The walls of Yo Mama's were covered with bright and lovely acrylic paintings of naked women in various poses and with various props, which emphasized their power.

The proprietor of Yo Mama's, Jerome, told us of the ten years he had spent homeless. He had been kicked out of his house at sixteen and was a crack addict. Jerome related a most amazing story. He admitted that he had been illiterate until Jesus found him destitute in an alley. There, in the alley, Jesus handed Jerome a Bible and commanded him to read it. Miraculously, Jerome could read from that moment on.

He played with remote-control cars while Leia and I, the only patrons in the shop at this late hour, conversed at a table in the cafe.

"Do you agree with Marx that marriage between a man and woman is simply a patriarchal convenience for identifying and keeping one's property?" I pondered over sips of a midnight cappuccino.

"I believe that life is for growing and learning lessons together. As partners," Leia, an artist, offered a more romantic counter theory.

"I agree that life is for growing and learning lessons, but a lesson of any value must be learned independently, for one's self. We're born alone, we live alone, and we die alone," I waxed eloquent.

"That's pessimistic, Boopsie!" Leia exclaimed.

"You accuse me of pessimism? You are the staunchest cynic I have ever known," I continued my argument. "And what do you know of relationships, Leia? You're a virgin. Now you're espousing romance? I will agree that those in relationships that break up have grown and learned a lesson. But I assert the lesson is self-sufficiency. When I see a couple holding hands as they walk down the street, I want to shout at them, 'EVOLVE!' Especially if they're wearing matching shirts."

Leia and I retired to the basement, where we found a tent set up in which we could sleep for the night. The coffee shop upstairs had long since closed.

"Go upstairs and get a candy bar," Leia requested.

I dragged myself up the stairs and asked Jerome for a Kit-Kat bar. He assented and turned away from me to retrieve the candy from the counter. It was then that I saw Jerome's crack-smoking, naked ass. I couldn't even believe what I was seeing. He was wearing a polo shirt. Nothing else. I squeaked, grabbed the candy bar, threw a dollar on the counter, and ran back downstairs, not bothering to collect the change.


Those were good times with Leia. To get the governess job in Chicago would be great. To roam the city streets with Leia again would be amazing. Nostalgia? Leia's not a virgin anymore. She's not even a lesbian anymore. The last I heard from Leia she was in a serious relationship with some guy. I'd like to meet him. Any guy who could tame Leia must be something else.

In full confession, in addition to Leia, I have a sexy college professor in Chicago, Professor K——. I find myself longing for his embrace. Maintaining regular correspondence, Professor K—— signed the latest of his letters, "With Love, P. K——." With Love! During our acquaintance as professor and student, I had considered Professor K—— the nerdiest nerd in academia. Now, with time and distance, I have come to see that he is the coolest, hottest, most suave man in the world. I've matured and become a woman since we parted.

It is safe to conclude Professor K—— loves me romantically. Passionately. He is constantly in my thoughts, causing me to move through daily life as if in a trance. If this is love, it is quite unsatisfying due to the thousands of miles of distance that keeps us apart. In a way, it is also exciting. I self-stimulated using a note he sent me. I pressed my breastbone against the cardstock and thought about him. It did cross my mind in the moment that what I was doing was strange. Slowly, desire overtook any rationality and pulled the card clutched in my fingers down my body. I felt the smoothness of the paper on my skin. I tried to imagine the feel of Professor K——. Stopping my retelling there so as to spare new readers any feelings of discomfort would seem prudent.

---

The Smith family responded to my email. They wrote that she was a professor at a medical school. He owned a business. They wished to meet me in person for an interview. They would call me with an electronic confirmation ticket number for a weekend flight to Chicago to meet their lovely family. Attached to the email was a digital photo from the family's glacier cruise to Alaska. They wrote that this photo was taken shortly after Mr. Smith's brain tumor was operated on. They look like a happy family.

# Mrs. Smith

*JULY 13, 2002*

**M**rs. Smith picked me up from O'Hare International Airport with her youngest daughter, who I knew was named Emma. I located them immediately by spotting the expected cardboard placard with *'Boopsie O'Flannigan'* scrawled on it in black magic marker.

In real life, Mrs. Smith didn't look like she did in the family photo she had sent me via email. In the photo, she seemed like a pretty suburban housewife. Bland and a bit dowdy, as is seemingly inevitable after childbearing. In person, Mrs. Smith was long and lean, and carried herself with elegant sophistication. She did a good job of taking care of herself especially considering she had birthed children.

Mrs. Smith's face was unfortunately dominated by a beak of a nose. It was similar to what you might see jutting forth from the head of some exotic bird perhaps endemic to the rainforests of Madagascar. Her nose was long and thin, with receding nostril flaps that allowed an observer much more knowledge of her nasal passages than comfort would dictate. It so dominated her face that the space between the nose and the upper lip was negligible, causing her mouth to constantly be agape. The top front teeth within her sour puss were thereby always exposed. It was as if she were perpetually breathing through her mouth, despite what would seem the apparent adequacy of the nose to do the job.

Puckered so, Mrs. Smith's pale face was caked in powder and the light blue sagging under her deep-set black eyes probably and understandably developed after Mr. Smith's tumor. Other than the over application of foundation, she certainly wore her makeup well. But her nose!

What surprised me most about Mrs. Smith's appearance is that she dressed like a classy hooker. I'm often amazed by middle-aged women who manage their suburban kid-slinging lives with chicken legs in stiletto heels. Perhaps said middle-aged women would be amazed by my beefy legs, which allow me to scale 5,000 foot mountain peaks in running shoes whilst sporting a hangover. Mrs. Smith would explain later in the weekend that her best friend owned a boutique in downtown Chicago and dressed her at a steep discount. What kind of boutique, dear?

I immediately fell in love with the young girl, Emma. She was absolutely darling. Her straight blond hair was extraordinarily long for a two-year-old child. A round little porcelain face served as an adorable frame for her bright blue eyes. In short, Emma bore the appearance of a Rubenesque cherub. I could see myself becoming quite attached to her in very little time.

Propped on her mother's hip, Emma scrutinized me with a discrimination beyond her years. I presumably passed her inspection and she reached out to me with both of her arms. Mrs. Smith handed the child to me whereupon the girl comfortably latched onto my hip. The mother was clearly pleased the girl and I had bonded so well and so fast.

Mrs. Smith led us out to the parking lot of the airport. Her stacked, silver Audi station wagon was filthy within. Papers, fast food wrappers, toys, clothes, all cluttered her luxury automobile. An overwhelming stench of sour milk slammed my senses as I entered and settled into the front passenger seat.

"This car is on lease," Mrs. Smith said.

"Oh," I managed to utter, shocked and at a loss.

"We have a Toyota Camry for you to drive."

"Okay." I was again at a loss.

*You trust me already to drive your vehicle?* I thought. *What is more, you trust me to drive your vehicle with your children in the car?* At that point, so soon upon meeting, and my fitness for the job a question of focus, I couldn't reveal to her that the village I grew up in had only two paved roads and no stop lights. I couldn't tell her that I'm simply terrified by the thought of driving in Chicago. I couldn't tell her that I didn't even know what most traffic signs indicated.

"Are you a doctor at the hospital?" I asked to break the awkward silence.

"Not that kind of doctor. I have a Ph.D. But I do teach medical students. I'm currently working on a study concerning the effectiveness of combining cancer drugs."

When she spoke, despite her squeaky and nasal voice - clearly a casualty of her enormous nasal cavities - I could discern Mrs. Smith's sharp intelligence. She was an erudite and sophisticated woman.

*I believe that I can grow to respect Mrs. Smith. Can a fiercely independent woman respect a married woman? Yes. The fact is, I respect a number of married women. What is most important to inspiring such respect is that she holds the deepest respect for her husband. A married woman who dominates her husband is a woman who settled for a man who was not her equal. Whose Mama taught her to settle? A married woman who is to gain the respect of her independent sisters, is a woman who married a respectable man. A man who loves his mother, but not too much. A man who cherishes women for their inner beauty, strength, and intelligence, but knows how to make a woman cum. Such men as these are few and far between, which is why so many of us women remain independent. There are few men who are our equals.*

"I'm so glad Emma likes you." Mrs. Smith said excitedly, sounding sincere. "I'm sure our daughter Mandy will like you too. I also have another daughter, Annie, who is your age. She is working for SETI, which is the *Search for Extraterrestrial Intelligence*. That is a NASA project searching with satellites for signals from extraterrestrial civilizations. Annie is a genius. I think that Emma will be too. Mandy…" Mrs. Smith's hesitant pause was telling. "Mandy is more like her father."

# Mr. Smith

**M**rs. Smith steered us into a squeaky-clean suburb. Grand lawns with tidy landscaping led up to modest mansions in Tudor and Georgian architectural styles.

"This is the neighborhood where John Hughes filmed the movie, *The Breakfast Club,*" Mrs. Smith narrated as she drove.

The car stopped in a cul-de-sac where there were situated more fine examples of turn-of-the-century mansions of which the neighborhood was so prevalently populated. I was quite impressed with the exterior of the Smith's house, but walking further up the driveway, I was confronted with pots filled with dried-up and long dead flowers. *Mrs. Smith doesn't garden? How hard would it be to give the plants a little water?*

Mr. Smith opened the door as I approached the threshold. He looked like what I expected from the family photo, except for the four inch square patch of missing skull where his scalp sunk inward forming a glaring indentation. I had been told he had surgery for a brain tumor, therefore, my only surprise was that the removed portion of his skull hadn't been replaced afterward.

From what I could garner through visual observation, Mr. Smith was past middle age and pasty white. He carried some pudge around the stomach, which he must've been battling with limited success. Male pattern baldness framed the conspicuously large dent in the right side of his frontal lobe. What hair hadn't yet succumbed was dark brown, with only a little gray (considering what he had been through). He wore wire-rimmed glasses, which were a bit oversized for his square face. The silver glasses cast a glare that detracted from his small, brown squinty eyes.

Standing barefoot on the top step of the porch and dressed in khaki shorts and a yellow polo shirt, Mr. Smith extended his hand to me in a gesture of welcome greeting.

"Hello! You must be Boopsie." Mr. Smith's voice was friendly and struck me as quite similar to Kermit the Frog's voice. His smile was genuine and a bit crooked. "We're really happy to meet you. Thank you for coming."

Mr. Smith opened the door to the house and signaled for me to enter ahead of him.

*Mr. Smith is at once charismatic and charming. I expect my respect for him to only grow. I already like him immensely and we've just met. He seems to be that rare kind of middle-aged man that a young woman could consider a friend.*

*I assume because Mr. Smith has some hair and plenty of spare mass, he is no longer in treatment for his brain tumor. I am too well-mannered to ask, and no one in the know has volunteered any recent information as to the status of Mr. Smith's health. I have almost come to terms with being a servant. I know that because I am simply a servant to these people it is not within my bounds to ask such personal questions. What information is not offered is not mine to know.*

*'O'Flannigans should work for no one but themselves' is an aphorism in my family. In my new position as a governess, I am breaking with the generational wisdom this aphorism represents. I am, however, informed of the customs and manners gleaned from my scholarly perusal of Victorian literature. Who better to learn of servitude from than the gentlemanly and refined Victorians? Indeed, it is not within the bounds of my position to ask if Mr. Smith still suffers from cancer, if he is in remission, or if he is completely cured. All I can hope is to glean this from his appearance. From his robust physique, jovial manner, and by the lack of any hint that he is still suffering other than the massive dent in his head, I gather Mr. Smith is well.*

"Boopsie O'Flannigan, meet my daughter, Mandy. Mandy, this is Boopsie." Mr. Smith's introduction to the eldest child was rather formal but spoken in a friendly tone.

The nine-year-old Mandy appeared lanky and freckled. Her dark-brown hair was well down her waist at the back and cut in blunt bangs across her forehead. I found it cute that she wore a retainer, which caused her to speak in an adorable lisp. I anticipated getting along with Mandy well. I would very much like to be a role model to this awkward girl as she matures. She greeted me immediately with a hug. I took her warm embrace as a good sign. My first impression of Mandy was that she was a great girl.

"You won't meet our dog, Tooty this weekend. She's at the veterinarian," Mandy lisped through her orthodontic device.

"Too bad. I hope she's well." I tried to sound concerned.


That night, when the children and Mr. Smith were asleep, Mrs. Smith guided me through some family photo albums. She showed me a picture of her first-born daughter, Annie. Blonde, curly-locked Annie. With an ivory face, a pretty smile, and no trace of her mother's nose.

"Annie is so pretty and smart and popular. Annie is perfect. I worry that Mandy feels inferior to her," Mrs. Smith confided to me.

After a moment of stunned silence I said, "Mandy is wonderful too." Because of this exchange, I decided I would love Mandy. The poor girl's mother thought she was second best. Young Mandy needed a grown woman in her life for whom she was the apple of her eye.

I got to see Mrs. Smith and Mr. Smith's wedding photos. As one might expect, Mrs. Smith wore a cliche satin wedding gown with enormous puffy sleeves. Her bangs, sprayed into an equally enormous wave, give the irrefutable indication that they were married in the eighties. What was more, Annie must be ten or twelve in the pictures. Did the couple wait many years after giving birth to their first child to get married? Or was Annie a child from a previous relationship? Was Mr. Smith her second husband? I remembered my Victorian manners and said nothing.

In the still house, I picture the vastness of the city around me, and I can sense its frenetic pace. Chicago nights cause profound sadness in my heart. They always have. I am in awe at the Smith's beautiful home, furnishings, and vehicles. I've tip-toed to the attic bedroom designated as my space. The sheets patterned with pink and brown roses match the wallpaper in perfect replication. I realize that I could never have these expensive things for my own. I am a simple governess. Perhaps my wise and cheerful uncle was correct. O'Flannigans should not work for other people.

I joined Mrs. Smith as she performed Emma and Mandy's bedtime routines. I was surprised she had to cajole Mandy to brush her teeth, but I reasoned the retainer must hurt her mouth so that the child resisted inserting the brush.

Mandy was older so she read to herself while Mrs. Smith read to Emma. That night she read *Goodnight Moon* in the original French. Emma was precocious and taught herself to read at only two and a half years old. Most kids were learning to string together a few words of English at her age. Mrs. Smith was teaching Emma to speak French. I was impressed. After turning out Emma's light, we joined Mandy in her room.

Mandy reclined under the covers with her head propped on feather pillows. She was reading a *Children's Encyclopedia of Dogs*.

"Boopsie, thank you for swimming with me today," Mandy lisped reflecting on the day's activity in the large backyard pool. "It was so much fun. The last woman couldn't swim."

Mrs. Smith, seated at Mandy's side, stared down unmoving.

Positioned at the foot of Mandy's bed, I said, "I should be thanking you, Mandy. I don't get many chances to swim." I tried to not skip a beat cheerily adding, "The water is too cold in Alaska!" I resorted to cliche to cut the tension, but I was inwardly processing Mandy's comment. Who was 'the last woman?' Why wasn't she caring for the Smith children any longer? Why didn't Mandy use her name?

When Mandy was tucked in, her book closed and set on the bedside table, and her nightlight switched on, Mrs. Smith gave her a kiss on the cheek. Mandy asked me for a kiss as well. I paused, but decided it boded well for my job prospects and complied. Mrs. Smith and I descended to the living room to join Mr. Smith.

The living room of the Smith home was large and lavishly furnished with a surprisingly funky flair. Along the far wall was a fireplace tiled in hot-pink. The carpeting was soft and featured a zebra-stripe pattern. I was taken aback by the Smith family custom of wearing their shoes inside the house. Most families I knew removed their shoes when they entered a home. I was horrified I would track in bubble-gum or poo and stain the exquisite black-and-white carpeting. Above the shockingly pink mantle hung a black and white photo of a Weimaraner wearing a trench coat. I was aware of the specific dog breed depicted in the photo, as Mandy had told me earlier in the day while we played a friendly game of *Chutes-and-Ladders*.

The unexpectedly eccentric furnishings contradicted the classical Georgian exterior in the averagely uniform neighborhood. They gave the home personality and gave me the impression the Smiths were more laid-back than formal. Nevertheless, I was deliberate in my movements and posture as I sat upon one of the large and fluffy yellow couches. Mrs. Smith sat beside Mr. Smith on the other.

"We would like to get to know you better, Boopsie," Mrs. Smith began.

"And we would like for you to know us too," Mr. Smith added.

"I would like that as well," I affirmed. I maintained a friendly smile, but I felt stiff and couldn't relax despite the ultra-soft cushions beneath me. I hoped my awkwardness wouldn't show.

"So, tell us about yourself," Mr. Smith said with a friendly smile. Mrs. Smith nodded.

"Well, I grew up in Alaska. Growing up in an isolated and bleak little town, I knew there was more to the world." I wondered if I was hitting the mark. Were they judging me? I continued, "In retrospect, I appreciate how life in rural Alaska has shaped me. Because of my upbringing in the Arctic, I love nature and I'm not superficial or materialistic. I understand what life is really about, I think." Then I got to the point. " That being said, I've always wanted to see the rest of the world."

"We love to travel," said Mrs. Smith. "We've been all over the world together."

"We're planning trips to Egypt and China. Egypt is on my bucket-list," Mr. Smith chimed in.

"Wow! Amazing," I earnestly replied.

"What did your parents do in Alaska?" Mr. Smith asked.

"They were both school teachers," I said, adding, "Alaska has great schools. In the eighties Alaska was flush with oil money. The state used it to attract and retain the very best teachers. I benefited from an excellent education."

"I grew up here in Chicago," Mrs. Smith volleyed. "My family is Polish and very Catholic. My parents always wanted me to be a nun." She smirked.

"Wow," I managed to reply.

"My niece is eighteen and wants to be a nun," Mrs. Smith shook her head and rolled her eyes at her own comment as if it were absurd.

Mrs. Smith wore an air of indignation seemingly at the thought of a young girl devoting herself to a spiritual life. As if, in this day and age, it was a sort of mad martyrdom to turn away from worldly pursuits. I, however, empathized with the girl's ambition as it were. I let slip a theory that had been rolling around in my head for some time.

"I consider myself a sort-of nun," I said and received a response of blinking eyes across from me on the fluffy yellow couch.

Understanding I had committed a faux pas, I tried to clarify my position. "I'm in service to some creative force. God, or the universe, or whatever you want to call it." Continuing, as I sensed I was not hitting the mark, "I want my life to be a statement of love, and I want to work selflessly for the good of humanity."

I didn't add that I like to fuck for God too. It wouldn't have been appropriate. I had studied tantra thoroughly and viewed sex as the ultimate creative act, a most sacred prayer.

"I just don't see the need to take vows," I tried to explain further.

The Smith's nodded graciously. "Okay," said Mr. Smith, cutting the tension. In his frank manner he got to the point of the conversation. "Listen, Boopsie. We think you're perfect." The Smith family formally extended an invitation to move to Chicago and work for them. I was told to be back in Chicago in two weeks. We would be traveling to Budapest together in three weeks.

# Alice

JULY 26, 2002

**B**idding me farewell, Alice took me out for a lunch of pizza and beer. Ever a source of sage advice, Alice spoke. "Listen, I like the idea of you traveling and seeing the world. You will no doubt learn a lot. I'm a little worried, though, Boopsie. It's fucked up if they can't take care of their own children."

"Yeah," I conceded. "But they're important professionals. Maybe they're cool, but super busy with their research and business. Or maybe they need extra support because of the brain tumor thing. That would be completely understandable."

"It'll be an experience and no doubt you'll learn something. Just be yourself and get out of there if it gets weird. You can always come home to Alaska. And write to me regularly," Alice instructed. "I look forward to reading of your adventures."

Finished with our fare, Alice and I went to a sex shop. This particular sex shop was clean and located in a respectable central Anchorage strip mall, so we needn't sulk nor feel dirty for our patronage. Whilst inspecting the various pleasure devices, a strange couple creepily consulted with us, suggesting we check out a website they insisted had 'the best toys.'

"Uh, huh. Yeah," Alice and I replied in near unison, trying not to engage them further. Alice and I looked at each other knowingly. A conversation of mutual disdain was exchanged through our eye contact. We were confused for lesbian lovers again.


Alice and I met on the first day of Sophomore English in high school. She was the new teacher. Alice taught our class to appreciate Greek literature, modern classics, and lovingly fostered my passion for Victorian literature. The summer of my high school graduation, Alice asked me if I could get her some marijuana. Of course, I could, the best stuff in the village. After the apportionment of which we became very close friends.

We lived as roommates in Anchorage for two years while I finished university and she saved up to buy a house. Alice and I knew everything about each other. We knew each other's greatest secrets. We knew each other's kinks. The best talks we had were about sex, being single and carefree women, and the pessimism and inevitable disappointment that was the result of sex with men.

Though critical of men, Alice revolted at the thought of lesbian sex. She was famous in her family for extemporaneously spouting to her mother over a fine dining experience, "I like a thick cock."

"Me too," was her mother's reply.

I don't think Alice would judge me if I did become a lesbian. Perhaps, however, a lesbian relationship would be as disdainful to her as a heterosexual relationship. You see, Alice was simply anti committed relationship. Period. To be a sexy, independent woman was what Alice taught me to strive for most in this life. Perhaps a lesbian fling with no expectations and no strings attached would pass her favor.

Blonde and beautiful, Alice was eleven years older than me. She was my teacher in worldly and spiritual affairs. She was studying to be a yoga teacher and I considered her my guru. Under her guidance, I had grown from a nihilistic and painfully self-conscious adolescent into a socially responsible and sexually expert anarchist.

Don't fret gentle readers, I'm no longer a nihilist. I believe in social responsibility. I believe in a social order that is impelled by each individual's sense of right, rather than one compelled by an external authority. I believe in the inherent goodness of human beings and that, if allowed true freedom, we would all choose to act appropriately and with an innate sense of morality and justice. I am taken with the difference between freedom and liberty. Freedom is our birthright from God. Liberty is what is allowed you within the confines of the shackles of the laws of men.

Alice and I had deep philosophical discussions. She encouraged me to self-examine and develop my intuition. She nudged me toward attainment of my full potential. It was a spiritual relationship toward self-actualization. We also had the slap-happy adventures of hardcore stoners.

I remember one episode when we had a wake-and-bake session before a planned Saturday morning hike through the mountains that tower behind Anchorage. When it was time to load ourselves into Alice's Volvo station wagon, she couldn't find the car keys. After searching the entire house, she started to panic, presumably thinking she'd been robbed of her car keys.

"Boopsie, should I call the police?" Alice asked with urgency.

"Don't call the police, Alice," I implored her. "We're both stoned out of our gourds."

"I think I should call the police," she said with unchanged urgency.

After some convincing, she agreed not to call the police. When the munchies hit, she found her car keys in a bag of potato chips. *That episode was stoner gold. It still makes me laugh to think about it.*


Managing to shake-off the confused and creepy older couple at the sex shop, I decided upon the purchase of a large shiny silver vibrator with a clear, rubbery, plasma-like coating. It was waterproof and much too large for my body, I would soon realize after bringing it home, disinfecting and christening the device, Johnny Rocket. Maybe I could grow into it?

"Take your new vibrator on your trip, Boopsie," Alice commanded in the tone I recognized as that of a guru imparting sacred tasks unto the young seeker.

"Of course, I will," I replied. "I bought this silver beauty to secretly entertain myself while I am away living the life of a prim and proper nanny in Chicago."

"No, I mean take it on your trip with them to Budapest."

My mouth was agape, and my eyes widened. "But I'll have to pass through customs!"

She smiled maniacally. "I know!"

"What if customs takes the damned thing out to inspect such a strange mechanical object? What if the Smith family sees it? If all its erotic glory was exposed to the world, I might feel weird about using it again".

"It could happen," Alice warned. Smiling, she did not relent on her command.

We both cackled in delight.

# Read Jane Eyre



*JULY 29, 2002 (SOMEWHERE OVER THE CONTINENTAL UNITED STATES)*

Sitting on the plane gives me time to write. Thank you, kind diary for being such a wonderful listener. I will try to write more frequently as I make my new life in Chicago. How bittersweet to be leaving my homeland. I have never before left my home state but for an aborted attempt at attending a private college. Every friend I have ever made, excepting Leia, is to be left behind. But nearness to Professor K—— awaits me.

Alice will be sorely missed. She had been my guide in life, my constant companion these last few years at the state university. She had been my entertainment and my shoulder to cry on. My moral support and my guru in vice. Together in mountaineering and dildo shopping alike. She had been my wing-man in search of joyous sex and my comfort when such attempts are in vain. After all we have been through, Alice and I will always be part of each other's lives. I am forever devoted to her. She is my guru.

Why, even upon my departing for this trip to Chicago, Alice made an assignment for furthering my self-development. "Read *Jane Eyre*," she commanded. "You'll think it's funny."

And so I shall, Alice. I will miss Alice's deep wisdom and bawdy humor. She made a profound and lasting impression upon my soul. However, won't it be great to step out on my own in this wide world? To have no one to rely upon but myself would be the greatest condition toward refinement of soul. 'We are born alone; We live alone; We die alone,' it is said. In this sense, what a crutch my relationship with Alice has been! And what an extraordinary amount of marijuana we have together smoked! Yes, to step away from my dearest friend and strike out to live with only myself to rely upon will be a true test of character. This is a wonderful opportunity to perfect my soul. After all, hasn't the focus of every teaching I have received from Alice been that of independence? Independence from dependency to any man, yes. But further beyond the surface, the truest sense of her lessons were independence from any other person. All dependent relationships are a crutch. This I firmly believe.

Professor K—— once pontificated, "A year of travel will teach you more than a lifetime of books."

That line made a deep furrow in my heart. Since my youth in a small frozen village, an overwhelming curiosity for the wider world has filled my imagination. The isolation of my remote home had been demoralizing and depressing. I can no longer ignore the call of my heart to know something more of the world.

Professor K—— was also calling to my heart. His simple correspondence of two months ago was motivation enough for me to pledge eternal devotion. Living with the Smith family, I will be mere miles from his residence on the campus of the educational institution where we met. He will surely be happy to be so near to me again.

He signed his last letter, "With Love." I think I am correct in inferring this statement to be a pledge of love! This is not a leap of fantasy. I recall the time when he was my professor and he would take me to lunch.

We would get burritos from a not-so-nearby Mexican restaurant. He would pick me up from the dormitory in his powder blue Geo and away we would go. I was a shy type and had no idea that an older sophisticated man such as Professor K— would have intentions other than cultivating an innocent rapport between professor and student.

On one of our outings, Professor K— confessed that I was his best student. I assumed he respected my scholarly pursuits. I assumed he was thinking of my brain, my reason, my writing. Only recently had I pieced together what was truly transpiring those three years ago. Oh, how could I not see it then? To me, to my eighteen-year-old eyes, he was skinny and nerdy, but also older and my superior, to be held in the highest respect. Not at all a man to consider licking and sucking on and such sordid things.


But now I see. Oh, yes! I shall at last be near Professor K— again, and he will no longer see me as a girl. He will behold me grown, a woman of worthy vocation. A woman with longings. A woman with needs.

Also to be considered as I make sense of this new undertaking, I am in debt. The Smith family offered me a generous salary of four hundred dollars a week, which after a month and a sufficient evaluation would be raised to five hundred dollars a week. This entire sum can be applied toward repayment of my student loan, as room and board is also a part of the package. In addition, health insurance will be provided, and though I am the picture of health, one can never be too careful.

I vow to pay off my student loan and save enough money to travel the world. I vow to travel to the places the Smith's don't take me. To be honest, I have never felt a real drive to see Budapest. I know nearly nothing of the place. However, I do have irresistible longings for other parts of the world. I would especially like to see Greece, Mexico, and Australia.

How I adore Greek literature! It seems my life would not be complete until I have seen the land from whence sprung Aristotle. How I impressed Professor K— with my unique interpretation and criticism of his beloved Aristotle. Perhaps Professor K— might escort me to Greece.

Likewise, I feel deeply driven to the sacred sites of Mexico. Especially of interest were the ruins of Palenque, infamous for the psychedelic mushrooms which reportedly abound in ditches alongside the roads. Palenque will be my first foray when I have saved enough money. I also hear much about Australian men, and marsupials are adorable animals, that I could not in good conscience leave it off of my list! Certainly, I was not in error in accepting this position with the Smith family. It will allow me to see the world and thereby be an opportunity to better myself in every conceivable way.

I very much respect Mr. Smith. Surely I will consider him a friend. Mrs. Smith is such a worldly woman. I will take this opportunity of living with her to absorb from her what sophistication I am able. It could be I will learn about makeup and cosmopolitan beauty from her. I am already fond of the girls, Emma and Mandy. I will devote all of my attention to creating an unbreakable life-long bond between us.

# Chicago



*JULY 29, 2002*

Today was my arrival in Chicago to begin my new life as a governess to the Smith family. Mr. Smith and Mandy picked me up from the airport. They greeted me with vigorous hugs. Having sent my most loved books and other valuable but not immediately needed possessions via US Post, all the luggage I carried with me today were two heavy backpacks of necessary clothes, toiletries, books, and my guitar in its black case.

Mr. Smith expressed pleasure at the sight of my guitar case and informed me that he had a twelve-string guitar that he 'picks-around.' He said he would be very pleased to jam with me sometime. I smiled nervously.

Jamming with Mr. Smith I vowed inwardly to avoid. I tried to play and had many lessons and some technical knowledge. However, I hadn't the gift of musicality. I did put together an act for a college show, but it was an art-punk improvisation lamenting of STDs and scorn. Not at all appropriate for entertaining my young charges, I was sure. Despite not making much of Mr. Smith's request of mutual music making, I noted to myself that he was a bit more familiar with me than custom might dictate.

On the walk to the airport parking garage, I engaged Mandy with questions about her summer vacation. She attended equestrian camp and it was indeed fun, she confirmed with a metallic grin. I related to her that I did some wrangling in my youth. Other pleasantries crossed my lips. Mr. Smith led me to the airport valet where his convertible BMW was promptly retrieved. How grand was his life! I reflected upon the humble lifestyle I had lived until this afternoon. Strangely, I felt superior. My people retrieved their own cars. *Yes, independence is of the utmost*, I thought to myself.

As Mr. Smith drove us home, I struggled to converse, not wanting to seem the hillbilly that my rural upbringing might logically suggest. I hoped to convey to Mr. Smith that I was intelligent. I wished to gain his respect. He pointed out some landmarks along our route. My suspicion that he wanted to develop a friendship with me was confirmed when he began to tell me some of his life story. He said he was born and raised in New York City. He moved to Chicago to attend university and eventually earned his Ph.D. Upon graduation he started a business and made a fabulous life for himself.

"I am especially proud to tell you that I am, by just about most measures, the most popular executive in my company," he boasted.

This admission didn't surprise me in the least. Mr. Smith came across as charismatic and pleasant. I could easily imagine he was liked by most who crossed his path.

Much to my surprise, and against the custom of the nature of our relationship as employee and employer, Mr. Smith also told me a bit about how he made his fortune.

"In the summer of 1994, I decided to attempt to prove a point to those who thought me unworthy of my Ph.D. conferral. I founded and personally capitalized a company specializing in the development of computer software. With hard work, calculated risks, well-selected partners, and the critical intervention of my genius wife, we managed to rapidly grow the business."

I considered this to be an exceptional admission. To tell me such information, Mr. Smith must've considered me more than a servant. I thought he respected me and wanted to be my friend, too.

*Dare I say how worthy of respect Mr. Smith is? Fate has smiled upon me by merging my path with this utterly respectable man. I hope he's beaten the cancer. I feel a pang in my heart. What if we become dearest friends and he becomes gravely ill? I picture myself at his bedside. I wait up all the night placing cold compresses on his head and faithfully refreshing them. It seems right to devote myself to this fine man and his dear family.*

Upon our arrival at the Smith family home, Mr. and Mrs. Smith declared they would carry my baggage up the three flights of stairs to my new attic abode. I ardently refused, but upon receipt of equally ardent insistence, I consented. Who was I to have my employers carry my bags? Merely a lowly servant. In the same vein, who was I to deny my employers' insistence? Having read enough Victorian literature I knew the answer to the apparent paradox. Being thereby aware of the intricacies of social niceties, I was sure I must consent to their wishes. I was sure this demand to carry my bags was simply their goodwill toward my having a wonderful stay as a guest in their house. It was a pleasantry for my arrival that would be the only one of its kind. I stayed with the young children whilst their parents labored with my heaviest backpack, each one holding two corners of my burden.

Imagine my grief when I heard a loud crash and Mr. Smith bellowed "OUCH!" What must the children have thought when I started laughing? Though I should've, I didn't admit to them that I had a regrettable trait of laughing at the most inappropriate times. A dark humor that delighted when someone clumsily hurt themselves. Schadenfreude is the term for my inoperable condition. It does not denote madness, nor is it an uncommon affliction. The age-old gag of a clown slipping on a banana peel pays testament to the fact that others' pain is paradigmatically funny. I managed to stifle my laughter and gather myself in time for Mr. Smith's announcement that he had hit his head on the landing while laboring with my cumbersome luggage.

"Oh, I'm sorry!" I empathized.

"Get me some ice," he grumbled his demand and retreated to nurse his head.

Much to my disappointment, Mrs. Smith informed me that I would be taking the children immediately to the neighborhood library for a magic show. I had no time to settle into my new quarters. Straight off the flight from Alaska to work? Oh, well, I hid my chagrin well and accepted this command from my new employer. Then I was struck by a wave of the heaviest dread. I would be driving for the first time in Chicago. This strange city with unfamiliar streets and unknown traffic laws. I hoped my anxiety didn't show.

I gathered the children in the car and followed Mrs. Smith's directions scrawled on an old envelope she found on the kitchen counter. I took a couple wrong turns, but we made it alive and well to the library. The magic show didn't hold the children's attention, but to my satisfaction I learned the way to the library and discovered I could use a public computer and access the internet there. The children and I returned home, and Mrs. Smith assumed responsibility for the girls.

---

I have retired to bed, and I am ready to pass out. I can sleep with contentment tonight as my accomplishment of driving in the city without crashing proves a great relief.

# The Land of Plenty



I awoke at 7:30 am. This was rather early for me. I showered and put on a touch of make-up and headed downstairs to see what awaited me. The Smith family were all awake and had fed on cereal I judged by the shambles left on the kitchen counter. I was confused. These people had not made themselves clear as to my duties. Should I have made breakfast for the children? I had been told nothing of the sort. In fact, I was told nothing of my duties, except that I was to be the girls' governess. Upon the stoop of the stairs of my room I had found a cookbook lying in wait at my arrival. Clearly this had been a sign they were expecting some responsibility from me in a culinary capacity. I would have liked it if they had been clearer with me. I especially would have liked to know when I am expected to rise. I felt odd that they had let me sleep in. I am the servant, after all. Shouldn't I have been the first to rise and see to it that the children rise?

I rifled through the cupboards in search of tea. I felt a bit awkward digging through the cupboards of someone else's house. I remembered Goldilocks as a cautionary tale against doing exactly this. The whole family was bustling in the dining room right next to the kitchen. What else was I supposed to do? I tried to think that it was my home too. Still, I felt like I wanted to be invisible and not intrude on their happy family life.

When my tea was made, only Mrs. Smith and Emma remained in the dining room. Mrs. Smith informed me that Mr. Smith was taking Mandy to her equestrian camp, and I would be expected to go to the grocery store. In fact, grocery shopping would be one of my regular duties. She instructed that I was to keep stock of staple items in the kitchen. Pleased that she had been clear with me about one duty, I was also again filled with anxiety about driving. Directions to the grocery store and a list of staple items which must be always in the kitchen were already posted with a magnet to the refrigerator. Mrs. Smith said I was to charge purchases to her account. She then said she was going to be working in her home office today and was not to be disturbed. She left me with Emma and the unbelievable mess in the dining room.

The dining room was as wildly funky as the rest of the house. Wallpaper printed to mimic yellow floor-to-ceiling drapes was hung on all four walls. The chandelier centered above the round hardwood table was flat white and featured miniature classical style busts bearing a likeness to Alexander the Great. I found it odd that the family used plastic cutlery and flatware. One might think they would use the finest china. Plastic plates, cups, forks, and spoons were on the shopping list of necessities.


Dressing Emma was fun. It was like having a pretty living doll to pick out clothes for. She screamed and cried for her mom when I tried to fix her hair. I thought it was a good idea that her unusually long hair should be kept up out of her face and I insisted on it. Finally, I found I must resort to light force, and I was glad I brought her up to my attic room for the chore. Her mother was less likely to hear her shrieks of displeasure from up there.

I strapped Emma into my new-to-me, used Camry, and off we went to the grocery store. It was painfully stressful being lost in a strange city with a two-year-old child in my charge, and with limited experience with urban driving. I managed to avoid a crash and to find the grocery store. Walking down the isles in the Land of Plenty, I saw possibilities in the arrangement of charging items to Mrs. Smith's account. I wondered if she is provided with an inventory of items I charge, or only the total price charged. I wondered how loaded the Smiths were.

Home again, home again. Emma cried for her mother, and it was all I could do to keep her from disturbing her mother's labors in the home office.


*Emma's crying is driving me mad. I wonder if her incessant crying will abate when she becomes used to me. In time, when we establish a routine and boundaries, Emma will not yearn to be with her mother who stays barricaded in her office upstairs. Mrs. Smith has insisted she not be disturbed. I have always been uncomfortable keeping a child from their parents. Who am I to separate families? The parent/child bond is the greatest force in the world and to come between it makes me terribly uneasy.*


Finally, Mandy returned from equestrian camp, and I could not have been happier. With her sister home, Emma was content, and her crying abated. Mr. Smith said hello and told me to make the girls lunch while he puttered about the kitchen making himself a ham sandwich. I learned that Mandy liked ramen noodles, "more than any other food in the world." Ramen noodles? Her parents could afford the finest food in the world, but Mandy developed a taste for ramen? I thought this may be yet another sign her mother was not a domestically inclined personality. I formed a plan to observe Mrs. Smith more to see if she was properly nourishing her children. Not that I would report the Smiths for neglect, only that I would like to know where to step in to give the girls all they needed to grow and thrive. I consented to ramen, but Mandy would also have to eat half a sandwich to round out her meal. In terms of preparation, ramen was easy for me. I wondered if I would be expected to make dinner.

*Again, I wish they would be clearer of their expectations of me. What would it take? A ten-minute conversation? But they don't even have time for their daughters. At least Mr. Smith drove Mandy to her equestrian camp. I think he must be a good parent. He just married a non-nurturing woman.*


Evening came and the Smiths relieved me of my duties with the children. I made use of the exercise room above the boathouse. They had nice exercise equipment up there and I planned to make good use of it on the regular. I hope to be in slamming good shape for our upcoming trip to Budapest. I ran for forty-five minutes on the treadmill and lifted weights for fifteen, followed up by my regular yoga routine. I tried using the TV in the exercise room to watch something whilst I ran, but I pressed a wrong button and it appeared I fucked-up the satellite settings. I ended up watching *Entertainment Tonight* on a local channel.

Later, in the kitchen, I found the remains of their take-out dinner. They left the plastic containers and remnants therein on the polished marble countertop. I supposed I am meant to clean up the mess. Easy enough. I found more take-out garbage on the dining room table. I supposed it would be my duty to clean the kitchen and dining room.

---

I am encouraged to have more clarity of my roles and responsibilities, though they must apparently be gleaned by deduction. I will be glad to keep order in the kitchen. After all, it's clear Mrs. Smith can't. I now see the benefit of using disposable dining ware. However, I wince at the thought of the quantity of garbage the practice produces. Just today the garbage can had filled to the top. The environmentalist in me is uneasy. I wonder what time they expect me to wake tomorrow morning?

# The Shedd Aquarium

*JULY 31, 2002*

I woke early but melancholy kept me in bed until Mr. Smith knocked at my door. That was uncomfortable. He yelled through the closed door that I would be late to take Emma to her Spanish class. Wouldn't it have been nice to know about Emma's Spanish class yesterday? I chose to forgo a shower and quickly dressed. Mr. Smith and Emma were downstairs in the dining room. Plastic chaos on the table served as evidence they had already eaten.

"Sorry we're rushing you. I forgot about Emma's Spanish class until this morning," Mr. Smith explained. "Mrs. Smith has taken Mandy to equestrian camp."

Mr. Smith's plan for the morning was for me to follow his car to Spanish class so that I would learn where the language school was located. It was to be my regular duty to deliver and accompany Emma in subsequent weeks.

Clutching the wheel of the Camry as I steered through the city behind Mr. Smith's silver BMW convertible, I almost vomited. I was nervous to drive under his gaze, even if only through his rearview mirror. What if I fucked up? What if it became blatantly evident I was an inexperienced driver? Surely they'd not let me drive with their children anymore. I would not be capable of carrying out the duties of my charge.

We arrived safely at the neighborhood's Jewish Community Center. Mr. Smith rolled down the window of his car, "When you get back to the house, you are to take Mandy and Emma to the aquarium for the afternoon."

"Okay," I replied.

Where was the aquarium?

Mr. Smith waved goodbye and drove away.

Emma's Spanish class was a fucking nightmare for me. I had no tolerance for adults who feign excitement and squeal to hold young children's attention. I find many people are intimidated by young children and feign a shrill excitement to cover their fear. Or they consider young children to be less than human, and exhibit a whiny, patronizing behavior. The Spanish teacher had the worst case of patronizing pedagogy I have had the displeasure of witnessing. It was intolerable. But to her credit, these very young American children were speaking Spanish when prompted. The students were suburban Jewish children, none of them older than three. I even learned some Spanish. Ciudad means city. After the lesson we drove home safely, and I fed Emma leftovers from the takeout her parents had ordered for lunch.

*The Smiths have ordered takeout for four meals since my arrival in Chicago. I have only been here for two days! I wonder if this is a sign I am neglecting my duty to cook their meals. No, I'm sure they would have said something if that were the case, despite the increasingly obvious fact they are shitty communicators. I still find it more likely Mrs. Smith is simply not domestically inclined.*

After cleaning the remnants of lunch, I was provided a brochure to the Shedd Aquarium. It featured a small map on the back flap I could presumably follow to locate the Aquarium. Mandy was extremely excited to go. She bounced around in her car seat and squealed as ten-year-old girls aggravatingly tend to do. If she had known about my terror of driving, she might not have been so excited. Mandy explained that she wanted to be a veterinarian when she grows up and there's nothing she loves more than animals. Despite the bouncing, I liked having Mandy around. Her presence made Emma much more agreeable.

Holy shit! Off we drove down Lake Shore Drive into the heart of the city! My heart pounded and my hands squeezed the steering wheel. We got lost and I had to ask for directions twice, but we made it nonetheless and that was quite an accomplishment for a girl from the village. Way to go Boopsie! *Now, where to park the Camry?*

The Shedd Aquarium was impressive for a city in the interior of the continent. Built in 1930, I learned the Shedd Aquarium was the second largest aquarium in America. Mandy was excited to watch the trained-seal show. She was quite taken with the hostess of the show. I found the hostess annoying. Not even an animal trainer, she was an actress and an annoying one.

"That's what I want to do when I grow up," Mandy asserted in a dreamy tone.

I said nothing in reply. Regardless of having to tolerate the annoying actress in big, stupid rain boots, I was impressed with the seals and happy to have come.

We had some time left so we walked around to view other exhibits. I empathized with the beluga whales kept in a small round tank. They were far from home, like me. The bright white whales seemed unhappy to be out of their native environment.

"They are so pretty!" proclaimed Mandy.

"They're pretty. They're also tasty with salt and pepper," I added.

I immediately regretted what I had half-unconsciously said when I saw Mandy's chagrin.

What if I had upset her? The people in my village ate beluga whales as part of their traditional lifestyle, but Mandy had an obsession with animals. What if she told her parents she didn't like me? I hoped she wouldn't tell her parents I recommended eating a cute, seasoned sea mammal.

Little Emma was hungry, so we left the aquarium. Anger flushed my face when I found a parking ticket on the windshield of the car. Not wanting Mandy to know I got a ticket, as I didn't want her parents to know I am an incompetent driver, I practiced kung-fu stealth. I secreted away the ticket, but Mandy didn't miss a beat.

"What's that?" Mandy asked.

"An invitation to return to the aquarium on another day." I likewise didn't miss a beat.

Making my way cautiously through the maze of roads in the city center, we stopped to dine at an unremarkable restaurant. The dinner was rather expensive considering the children ordered hotdogs and I a simple salad. I made a note to be sure to give the receipt to Mr. Smith for reimbursement. However, the Smiths were not to know of the parking ticket. It was of the utmost importance they continue to believe I am comfortable chauffeuring their children through the bustling streets of Chicago.

By some miracle of God, we made it home. The children were put to bed by Mrs. Smith. Mr. Smith told me I would have the day off tomorrow.

---

After exercising in the room above the boathouse, I am dead tired and ready for bed. My attic bedroom is a lovely retreat. Sloped ceilings afforded by the architecture of the roof add a cozy character. A spacious closet handily holds all my belongings and the attached bathroom sports a clawfoot tub. The most striking feature is the floor-to-ceiling wallpaper of pink roses to which are perfectly matched the sheets covering the soft single bed. It is a sacred space for me to retire, relax, and be alone. Despite living in a stranger's house, I do have a room of my own.

As I snuggle under the covers, I reflect. I'm in Chicago again three years after abruptly leaving college. I had intended never to return. Now I'm back and living with a beautiful family. I wonder what I should do with my free day tomorrow. Should I go to see Professor K——? He resides a few miles down Sheraton Road. He doesn't know I'm back in town. I did not yet alert him to my new situation in our correspondence. I don't think I should stop by unannounced. I've been thousands of miles away for three years. I don't know how he might take the surprise of seeing me and learning I'm living just down the road from him. I think I best write a letter explaining all of this before I go to see him in person. I think it best he have a bit of psychological preparation to allow him to get used to my returned proximity. Besides, written notice may allow him the pleasure of anticipation. Yes, I will write Professor K—— tomorrow. For now, Johnny Rocket, the big silver vibrator will do.

# Little Emma

❧



**M**andy had equestrian camp in the morning and was to be picked-up by her father for shoe shopping in the afternoon. I, therefore, would be with Emma all day. Emma tended to whine and cry ceaselessly when she was not with her parents or with Mandy. It was terribly awkward while her parents are working from home to have her crying within their earshot whilst she was meant to be in my capable care. When her parents heard her crying in my charge, did they think Emma didn't like me? Did they think I'm incapable?

The fact is young children, when given an option, would prefer to be in the care of their parents. It's natural. What nonsense, to a young child, that their parents are in the next room of the same house, and they should be kept away, sometimes with the necessity of physical intervention. Of course, in Emma's young eyes, I was the bad lady who kept her from being with her parents. Naturally, she wasn't going to like me. Added to this, I was a near stranger to her. We haven't had time to form a bond. I needed the Smith children to like me if this situation was going to work out.

Mrs. Smith's suggestion that I take Emma to their neighborhood beach struck me as a brilliant idea. Emma would be away from the house, and thus proximity to her parents, and maybe she wouldn't cry to be with them. Should she cry, the parents wouldn't hear and use it as an indication against my job performance. Plus, it was high summer. A cool dip in the lake would be most welcomed.

"Boopsie," Mrs. Smith said in a hushed tone, "you must promise me you will always be watching Emma at the lake."

Well aware of the potential danger, I assured her I would be at Emma's side for the entirety of our time at the lakeside.

"You see…" Mrs. Smith said haltingly with her head down. She took a moment to collect herself. Having regained her typical composure she said coolly, "My brother died from drowning in Lake Michigan, and I'm terrified of the water. I'm terrified of letting my children swim." She lifted her head to make unabashed eye contact. "Boopsie, you have to promise me you'll watch Emma at all times."

The seriousness of her request made clear, I understood my simple assurance hadn't been enough. To comfort her I changed tack. "Don't worry, Mrs. Smith. I was on the swim team. Emma will be safe with me."

She seemed relieved and I didn't elaborate. What remained unsaid was that I was a disaster on the swim team. It's not that I couldn't swim, dear readers, I simply wasn't good at it.


With shame, I remembered the swim meet my team flew to a bigger city to attend. The event was the 200m freestyle. I was on the blocks, the buzzer sounded to start the race, and I dove in and swam. They say a human brain is not fully developed until the age of 21. Swimming along, enjoying myself in the water, it hadn't occurred to my undeveloped brain that for a race I should increase my speed and swim like hell. I casually swam along at a comfortable pace, enjoying myself. The other contestants must have finished at least two minutes before I tapped out of the 200 meter swim. Imagine!

*However, now that I'm 23 and my brain is fully developed, I can see that event with a better perspective. The truth is, dear readers, I'm not a competitive person by nature. I don't have an 'Alpha' personality, I'm not 'Type A.' In fact,*

*I'm a Type Omega personality. I don't care about winning. I don't strive to be perfect. My aim is to just get by and enjoy myself doing it. Emma would be safe with me at the lake. We'd enjoy ourselves staying in the shallows.*


After my conversation with Mrs. Smith, regarding Emma's safety in the water, I packed a bag with all the items Emma and I would need for a day at the beach. She had the cutest little swimsuits and I let her choose which one to wear to the beach. Again, Emma and I had an argument over pulling her hair back. I managed, despite her screaming, to fix a quick ponytail. When I had finished with her hygiene, she looked back at me with disgust. Per her mother's request, I remembered to pack little inflatable floaties to be placed on the upper arms so that my charge wouldn't drown. Sunscreen, bottled water, and two peanut butter sandwiches were also neatly placed on the top of our tote.

Situated in a small upscale neighborhood on Lake Michigan, the Smith's house was within cycling distance to the water. In the boathouse, the Smith's had a collection of underused bicycles. I was given permission to use the oldest daughter's, Annie's, bicycle whenever I wanted. I loved bicycle riding. It was a favorite outdoor pursuit and I was happy to have access to a ride. I saw a bike trailer used to haul children among the bicycles and I decided to hook it up to Annie's bicycle and ride down to the beach with Emma in tow.

The beach was a few minutes away from the Smith's home and was very easy to find. What a marvel! Fine, light-brown sand lined the shore and happy children splashed in the clean waters of Lake Michigan. Rich people have it good. When I attended college, not too far from here, I would walk to Lake Michigan when I could. As an Alaskan, I commune with nature as a matter of spiritual necessity and Lake Michigan is undoubtedly the most natural element available in Chicago for communion.

Unfortunately, by the college campus, the shores of Lake Michigan were covered in dirty pavement. Most notably, and a recurring in my nightmares since, the view of the horizon offered from there, featured not only the perpetually chugging towers of a coal plant, but several chimneys of a massive nuclear reactor.

The great state of Illinois boasted of having the most nuclear reactors in North America. A good concentration of which were located in my college neighborhood. The potential hazard indicated therein didn't stop us brilliant college kids from climbing the concrete and having midnight dips in the lake. I joined a midnight swim once, dear readers, be assured, I learned my lesson. Following the late-night adventure, I was violently ill for days. I didn't know what real diarrhea was until I swam in Lake Michigan. I was later informed beaches in the area are closed periodically due to E. coli outbreaks.

For this Alaskan, Lake Michigan had not been associated with communing with nature. However, my beach day with Emma changed all that. We had a lovely day splashing in the shallows together. We dug and filled her sand pail to make sandcastle mounds and watched the them wash away in the gentle waves. As we ate our picnic of sandwiches and potato chips, Emma said sweetly, "Thank you, Boopsie. You're my best friend!" She hugged me with a rosy-cheeked grin.

Little Emma's rosy cheeks only got rosier as the day progressed and evening approached. I had not applied enough sunscreen, or it wore off in the water, or maybe the sunscreen was old and had lost its potency. Whatever the cause, Emma was badly sunburned, and it was my fault. Mrs. Smith was fuming. Mr. Smith did not ally himself with me in easing any tension the unfortunate matter caused. Yeah, I fucked up. But Emma didn't drown and at the very least, she didn't have E. coli.

*I'm not asking for kudos. Just cut me a little slack.*

## Evanston

## AUGUST 2, 2002

Having ridden Annie's bicycle to the university neighborhood of Evanston on a Friday night, I am sipping a mango smoothie and writing in this humble but faithful diary. Super-hip students walk past me. The intelligentsia converse about love making and dinner plans.

Sitting alone at a small table in front of the smoothie shop, I miss Alice and my tribe in Alaska. Does Alice know how much she meant to me? Will anyone here talk to me? Will I find a friend? Can I tame the will and win the heart of Emma? Will Mrs. Smith become more friendly? I do love Mandy. She is cheerful and amiable. Mr. Smith is a good man. I am glad to feel comfortable being around him despite our differing social status. Can I endure a year of this situation? Where are the heterosexual men? Will whoever owns that black cable-knit sweater left in the empty chair at the empty table beside me come back to claim it?

Earlier today, Mrs. Smith told me that she considered it my duty to make friends with other nannies in the neighborhood who have children Emma's age. Is was my duty to make friends? The order from her seemed questionable. I didn't voice my dubiousness though, due to my manners and the good humor afforded me by an earlier topic in our discussion.

"Before I met Mr. Smith," she said, "my grandmother wanted to introduce me to one of her friend's grandsons. She thought we would be a good match."

"Oh," I replied, not quite sure why she was telling me this and confused about what would be proper reaction to such a personal confession.

"His name was George," she continued, "George Clooney."

After an involuntary click of my tongue and a tilt of my head, I said simply, "Retrospect."

Mrs. Smith frowned and turned to another subject.

Perhaps my response had been inappropriate? Did emphasizing the clarity gained in retrospect imply she made a mistake in choosing Mr. Smith instead of George Clooney? Honestly, I didn't care what implications Mrs. Smith drew. I thought that I'd rather make friends with the nanny down the street.

Mandy and I brought the family dog, Tooty, to the dog groomer. It was eye-opening the way the dogs of the Smith's neighborhood were treated. The grooming shop itself was luxuriously furnished. Even the sofas and plush chairs where patrons waited whilst their canines were being washed and styled were lavish. Cushions laid upon the floor for the dogs to lounge whilst they waited for their allotted appointment were upholstered in rich textiles and stuffed with what was presumably goose down. I could only imagine the price of the cosmetic line with which little Tooty was lathered.

After the dog groomer, Mandy, and I picked up a freshly napped Emma and went to the neighborhood library. Taking advantage of a public computer, I used the internet to research the history of Hungary. I grew increasingly excited for the trip. I used Mrs. Smith's library card to check out a copy of *Jane Eyre* to bring with me.

*Dearest Alice,*

*Please excuse the lack of proper stationery. I am sitting in Evanston on a Friday night, drinking a smoothie and enjoying a cigarette.*

*I wonder if you know how grateful I am for your presence in my life and for teaching me what no one else could.*

*The Smiths are nice enough. It is awkward to be a servant, and to live in a strange house with strange people; but as per your instructions, I plan to read "Jane Eyre," and hope to learn my role as governess well. I suppose as time progresses and the Smith family and I become more familiar, the awkwardness will abate.*

*I think I shall be able to survive this role. However, for now this situation feels like a trial.*

*I'll write back when I have something more interesting to share.*

*Love,*
*Boopsie*


It was time to let Professor K—— know I'm in Chicago. We'd exchanged several letters over the years since I departed college. Surely this would be his favorite.

*Dear Professor K——,*

*You owe me a letter. I hope I haven't offended your sensibilities.*

*Somehow, since our last correspondence, I have come to be employed in Chicago as a nanny to two young girls. The family is intellectual and eccentric and travels frequently. I shall be able to see a bit of the world and pay off my student loans. If you wish to meet with me, I would be very happy to see you.*

*Faithfully Yours,*
*Boopsie O'Flannigan*


Money is an issue I need to face. I tend to spend money without thinking twice. Like anyone, I suppose, I want nice things. However, one of the reasons I am in this situation, living with the Smiths, is to save money. There is no need for me to get a mango smoothie every other day. Or for me to spend ninety dollars on a pair of designer jeans. Or effectively throw away twenty dollars on a cheap necklace.

Paying thirty dollars for a damned parking ticket from a damned aquarium and secretly paying it from guilt is probably not advisable either.

I should be open and honest with my employers about expenditures. I am nervous about giving my receipts to Mr. and Mrs. Smith for reimbursement for fear they will think me a profligate. Intensely hoping Mr. and Mrs. Smith don't find out about it, I secretly paid for the parking ticket from the Shedd Aquarium today. The ticket record is attached to a car which they own and registered in their name. I fear this incident will get back to them. If they discover how incompetent I am driving in a big city, they'll fire me. How useful to them could I be if I'm not capable of carting their children around?

I'm going to take the black cable-knit sweater abandoned on the chair next to me. I will close this diary, get up casually, and grab the sweater as I walk away as if it were my own. I will take it with me to Budapest.

# Leia



Last night I went into the city to see Leia. I drove into the heart of the city and survived. I was pleased with myself and beginning to feel like a capable driver. A capable woman with wild and wily friends. Leia was happy to see me, and as fun and fantastic as ever. I was glad my visit cheered her up. I had been worried about her as I had learned she was recently kicked out of the female artists' complex in which she was staying. A performance artist, Leia put-on a show considered too risqué and was told to leave the communal building. She called me a few weeks ago, before I had moved to Chicago, sobbing between outbursts of maniacal laughter. Reportedly, it was quite a show.

Being a classic Attention Deficit Hyperactivity case, Leia couldn't be beat in prolific art output. Not a day went by that Leia didn't find some profound way to share a bit of enlightened and spontaneous performance art with those who found themselves in her direct vicinity. On the night she was kicked out of the artist commune, Leia had put together a talent show. It would seem her new boyfriend got on stage and started slashing his body with broken glass. His public display of masochism was unplanned and unappreciated.

Upon seeing her boyfriend cut himself in front of her friends, peers, and housemates, Leia had a genuine and dramatic breakdown in front of the aghast audience. One would have thought that an apartment complex filled with progressive feminist urban artists would understand and even might've found deep meaning in Leia's boyfriend's performance. Perhaps a more thoughtful observer might even have experienced epiphany in contemplating this piece as an honest contribution to the creative expression of nihilistic performance art in the new millennium. But no. Leia was ejected from her accommodation and outcast from the community. A few of her loyal friends there were hiding her in their room despite her official shunning.

Since meeting Leia, it had been my wizened opinion she would either be famous, or in an insane asylum like her mother. I stood sure that the guardians of fate who sent Leia from drifting through various foster homes in Chicagoland to majoring at an acclaimed school of performance art would continue her trajectory and send Leia shooting to infamy. I couldn't wait to see her again.

After parallel parking with the greatest of pride and seeking assurances that no parking fee was required, I saw Leia watching me from the steps of her apartment building. She looked as unconventionally beautiful as ever. Her tight curls were dyed a bright fuchsia. Red patent leather combat boots clashed perfectly with her mustard yellow T-shirt on which was painted in Leia's hand *'DRINK MY PISS, YOU FUCKING DEGENERATE.'* Leia was a sight for sore eyes.

We ecstatically embraced and I told Leia her red and yellow look reminded me of Ronald McDonald. Not missing a beat, Leia commenced to perform an impromptu monologue as the character of Ronald McDonald's punk daughter.

"You think I want your chicken McNuggets, Dad? You think I want your BigMac, Dad? You can keep that toxic fucking shit, Dad." Leia gestured expertly as she entertained. "I'm a vegetarian, you see. You fucking pig."

Upon entering the lobby of the female artists' commune in which Leia was a hidden refugee, my eyes were immediately assailed

with fliers announcing the evening's happening at the collective - a
speed-dating event for Jewish singles. Cruel fate! That was my
dream event.


*Speed dating is a most brilliant invention, and I am pleased to be incarnate
during the times of speed dating. Who will deny that first dates are anything
other than interviews? Terrifyingly awkward interviews. To shorten this tortuous
convention into a matter of minutes is a thing of genius. In addition to shortening
the intervals of torture, a speed dater is able to meet, evaluate, discard, and
choose from scores of eligible men in one night. What woman is not delighted by
assortment and variety? Variety is the spice of life, they say. Added to this happy
event, Jewish men are on fare.*

    *I was raised Irish Catholic, but I find myself crossing paths with many
Jewish men. I lost my virginity to a Jewish man. Having despised all the men
I met in my redneck town, the sexual urges of puberty were controllable due to
lack of proper fodder. I was able to wait until I left my village and met a fine
specimen of human potential in the bigger dating pool provided in Anchorage. I
waited until I met a man my equal. A man of morals. A man of lofty goals.
A creative, and most importantly, compassionate man. I waited until I met
a Jew.*

    *Alas, not being Jewish myself, I am not eligible to participate in Jewish
speed-dating. This is discrimination! There is something not right that a beautiful single woman is not allowed to partake in the coupling with Jews.*


For a moment, I pondered falsifying my spiritual heritage and lying
to secure a place in that heaven-on-Earth. However, more pressing
matters were afoot. At long last, I was reunited with Leia.

Leia introduced me to Michelle, the curvy fashion designer in
whose cluttered room Leia was squatting. I also met Jill, the waifish
painter who engaged in frequent spontaneous threesomes with Leia
and her boyfriend.

Leia and I went together to the convenience store to get some
smokes and orange juice. It would be best we decided, to drive in
my Camry to Evita's apartment. Evita went to college with us. Like
many of our classically educated cohort, Evita found her niche and

fame in the sex industry. Evita was an internationally famous dominatrix. She also played the piano in Leia's artpunk band.

"How have you been doing, Leia?" I asked as I drove.

"Other than being kicked out of my apartment, I'm okay," she replied. " I feel that I am in a high place in respect to the development of my art. I'm also in love. You should come downtown tomorrow to meet him. He's performing in a play he wrote. It's a nihilistic play about the mafia and religion."

"I'm happy for you that you're in love. Really, Leia. But isn't it a little sick the way he cut himself up on stage? He's the reason you were kicked out of the collective."

"His play is getting good reviews," Leia assured me.

"Okay," I relented, trusting in her judgment. "I'm flying to Budapest with the Smith's on the morning after tomorrow, but I really want to meet your boyfriend," I said and then switched the subject. "What have you been doing for work?"

"You know how I was doing the foot-fetish thing?"

Leia had found, searching through the want ads, an advertisement for an adult worker to make loads of money - *'No sex required.'* She answered the ad and was hired by an 'agency' (a dirty old man in a dirty old office). The job was to meet men and let them worship her feet. No sex required. She had one regular customer and a few oddballs.

Leia continued, "The last time I said he could masturbate. When he started fondling himself I started lighting matches from a book of matches and flicking them at his dick while he was doing his thing."

"Ha!" I laughed in shocked surprise.

"While I was flicking the matches at him, I was singing children's nursery rhymes to him. Humpty Dumpty and shit."

It was good to see Evita again too. She was as beautiful as ever and seemed to be doing well for herself. She reported she was working as a dominatrix in a dungeon downtown. She made hundreds of dollars an hour beating men up as retribution for the millennia of oppression they have subjected women to. It was nice to know women like Evita were working for the cause. I was proud to consider these women as dear friends.

# Newcastle

**B**ecause I had been out in the city until late last night, I didn't think Mr. and Mrs. Smith would want me to go out tonight. I was pleasantly surprised to learn the situation was in fact quite to the contrary. This afternoon, I was begrudgingly sorting out Mr. Smith's laundry in the dusky basement when Mrs. Smith descended the stairs to speak with me.

"We're going to be on the airplane for a very long time tomorrow," she stated. "You should go out tonight."

The turn of events was ever so pleasing as now, with her blessing, I would be able to go into the city to see Leia's boyfriend's play. Encouraged by the way our conversation was thus far developing, I gained enough courage to give voice to a nagging question. "Mrs. Smith, why are we going to Hungary?"

"There is a scientist in Budapest whose work I respect," Mrs. Smith replied matter-of-factly.

"Ah, I see. Do you work cooperatively with him on your university research? It's nice that you are able to travel there to see him in person."

"No, Boopsie," she answered. "He is working on an experi-

50

mental treatment for cancer. We are going to have him work with Mr. Smith's brain tumor. I think he may be able to help us."

"Oh," I said with genuine interest. I never knew what to say to Mrs. Smith. She was stiff and made me feel awkward, like I wasn't good enough to be in her orbit.

Mrs. Smith elaborated, "The therapy he is developing has not been approved for use in the United States. We have to travel to Hungary for Mr. Smith to receive the course of treatment."

It was therein unfortunately confirmed that Mr. Smith was still sick with the cancer. I had been earnestly hoping he was well and had recovered from his illness. Despite the dent in his head, which served as irrefutable evidence of brain surgery, remained uncapped and presumably unfinished for quick access should further surgery be necessary, I had been hopeful he beat it. Learning this news, I was concerned for Mr. Smith. I was sad for the entire Smith family as well. Poor Mandy had been dealing with this morbidity lingering over the family's head all throughout her most formative years. Poor Emma might not even remember her father if he died before she was grown. Trouble woe, trouble woe!

Mrs. Smith continued, "I remember when I first started researching cancer drugs. I spent more time in clinical settings. Now I'm mainly in my office supervising research. But back then I was in clinics meeting patients and their families." She confessed, "I remember feeling pity for the families of patients. I remember being grateful I was not in their shoes. I can't believe I'm in this position now." In a moment of unexpected vulnerability, Mrs. Smith brought both her hands up and covered her face for a short moment. Revealing the magnitude of her torment, "Boopsie. It's really, really hard."

I was stunned by Mrs. Smith's candor. I wondered if she was going to cry. If she cried, I wondered, what would be the proper response for someone in my position? Should I hug her? Up until now, Mrs. Smith had been guarded with me and it's been clear she appreciated clear and proper boundaries in our roles as employer and governess.

The best reply I could come up with at the moment was genuine. "At least you're knowledgeable about these things. You're

the most capable partner anyone in his position could wish for.
You're an expert. If anyone can help Mr. Smith, it's you."

Mrs. Smith proceeded to tell me a bit about the experimental
remedy they sought in Hungary - the Newcastle virus. She informed
me that Newcastle virus was a disease carried by and affecting
mostly birds. The doctor they would be meeting in Budapest was
experimenting with infecting cancer patients with Newcastle virus as
a method of fighting the cancer. She elaborated, "The virus rapidly
infects the cancer cells, then kills them."

Sustaining direct eye contact, I nodded to indicate I was
following her explanation, and that I understood her explanation.

"His research is very promising," she continued. "But, for now,
this treatment is not approved in the United States. We will most
likely be making a few trips to Budapest in the next year or so."

I found it surprising that Mrs. Smith opened up to me. Especially concerning matters of such a personal matter. She seemed like
such an emotionally closed woman up until then. Her frank display
of vulnerability was a pleasant development. I wondered if she and
I would eventually come to forge a friendship. Something between
us shifted.

Despite our new familiarity, I didn't ask Mrs. Smith the obvious
next questions, 'Is Newcastle virus contagious amongst humans?
Could the virus spread from Mr. Smith to other people,
namely me?'

"You know, Boopsie, I …."

Just as our conversation had begun, it ended. Mandy stormed
into the basement looking for her mother. Mandy's long arms flailed
as she wailed. Tooty had bitten her.

I wasn't surprised Tooty bit Mandy. I had seen some shit.

Earlier in the week, Mandy gave me a tutorial on Tooty's care.
She showed me where the dog food was stored in the kitchen. She
told me how and when to prepare Tooty's two meals a day. Then
she demonstrated for me how she 'groomed' the Welsh Terrier.
*Hmmm…* I thought as I watched her wiggle her thumb and first two
fingers down deeply into the dog's coat at his neck and pinched. The
dog looked at the girl with a clear expression of annoyance. He
wriggled in her embrace. Then, *Oh fuck!* I thought, as the ten-year-

old girl twisted her wrist and ripped the fur out of the dog with a terrible force. He whelped and wriggled in a panic, trying to free itself from her hold.

"Tooty is untrained and disobedient," Mandy seemed to imply the dog was at fault. "But I was just a baby when my family got him."

*It was only a matter of time before that poor dog bit her. Frankly, she had it coming.*

# Wrigleyville

I met up with Leia at Evita's apartment in the city. The three of us went together to see Leia's boyfriend's play. Leia's boyfriend's name was Danny, but people call him D. Not Dee, just D.

The play D wrote and starred in was about a gay sadistic mafia thug who kidnaps the pope at the behest of his nihilistic lover in an attempt to start World War III. D played the character with gusto to a convincingly psychotic affect. That was the first time I'd met D, and after seeing his play, I was ready to declare with certainty that he was sick in the head. I was frankly worried about Leia being in a relationship with this guy. Sure, she was a strong eccentric, but he came across as unstable and dangerous.

After the play, Evita parted ways with us as she had men to dominate at the dungeon. D wanted ice cream, so I walked with him and Leia to an ice cream shop. It was funny that this big tough guy who, moments ago, I watched play an entirely convincing psycho ordered plain vanilla ice cream in a cone.

"Aren't you going to get an ice cream, Boopsie?" D asked.

"No. Ice cream makes me vomit," I abashedly confessed. "It's the lactose or some fucking thing. Ice cream doesn't sit well in my stomach and comes back up. I don't know, it's weird."

"C'mon, Boopsie," Leia goaded. "We'll puke with you".

I relented. Their eyes widened when I ordered an ice cream sundae.

"What the hell?" I shrugged. "I'm going to puke it up anyway."

Making conversation I asked, "So D, are you from Chicago?"

"No. I grew-up in Missouri."

D did in fact look like he grew up on a farm and was whelped on corn and bacon. He was rounder than I expected. The back of his head had a roll of pudge bulging around the top of his neck. He was pasty white, and black framed nerd glasses rested precariously on the end of his pug nose. Presenting himself as a proper nihilist, he was dressed all in black. D's jeans sagged at the butt, but not in the manner of inner-city fashion. They sagged because he clearly needed a larger size of pant at the waist but didn't have enough butt to fill-out the pant in the back. I was taken by surprise when I noticed he wore Converse shoes, as wearing popular name brands seemed counter to a nihilistic lifestyle.

"You're a nihilist?" I probed.

"Yeah," D affirmed.

"That means you want the world to end? Like in your play."

"I guess. I mean, I think everything is fucked up. You can see that, can't you? And doing anything is not worth a damned thing."

"I don't see that," I replied. "I mean, at the very least, there's the pleasure principle. Things are worth doing because they induce pleasure."

"Well, Boopsie, look at Evita. Men pay her thousands of dollars to induce pain. What the hell does pleasure have to do with anything?"


After finishing our ice cream, the three of us walked back, retching along the way, to the Smith's black Toyota Camry. Friends will not judge you for puking in public, but only true friends will puke along with you.

"You're alright, D," I voiced an end to my concern that Leia was with this guy.

We paused our trek for a moment, as D had to pee. He pissed into a garage someone left open.

Now, I'm an Alaskan girl and I therefore urinated outside on the regular. In fact, I often felt cleaner peeing in the woods than I did peeing in a public bathroom. However, pissing into a stranger's garage was a step too far for me. I was aghast.

"Will you touch my penis?" D asked me as he zipped up his baggy pants.

"No!" I exclaimed, realizing I needed to establish boundaries with this guy.

Thusly bonded over ice cream and vomit, the three of us drove to Wrigleyville, the proud home of the Chicago Cubs. D sat in the front passenger seat and directed me as I drove to a techno bar he knew. We found a parking spot at a McDonalds near the bar. Before exiting the car, D asked again if I would touch his dick.

"Jesus, No!" I said.

I had been aware that Leia and D had threesomes periodically, and I didn't judge her for it. It's just not my thing. Even if it was my thing, Leia was my best friend, and I would never complicate our relationship with sex. Let alone three-way sex.

Much to my chagrin, Leia supported D's request. "D is a good lay," she promulgated.

"He must be. He converted you from lesbianism," I said.

D chimed in, "I still can't believe she was a lesbian."

It was true though. When Leia and I were students at college together, she had been a virgin. Since my unplanned and sudden return to Alaska, she had at least two relationships with women.

"Really, D," I acknowledged with respect, "I find it utterly respectable that you've managed to convert a woman from lesbianism. You know what I mean? Who can please a woman better than a woman?"

D replied matter-of-factly, "I can."

"He can," Leia confirmed and laughed.

Continuing the conversation with a topical confession, I told them I once gave a guy a blow job and he said it was so good that he couldn't cum.

"That's not possible," Leia said dubiously.

"I believe it," D said curtly with conviction.

Elaborating, "He was a poet and a waiter. I grew tired of him quickly. When I broke up with him he wrote me a poem."

I recited the poem from memory.

*"Boopsie O'Flannigan*
*I*
*Expected*
*More"*

Leia chimed sarcastically, "Cute."

*Scenes from the Camry:*

D: Why don't you suck my dick like that?
BOOPSIE: Because you're my best friend's boyfriend.
LEIA: Do it.
BOOPSIE: No! This is absurdity.
D: What would it take to make you suck my dick?
BOOPSIE: Sorry pal. You see, regardless of the fact that you're my best friend's boyfriend, you're not my type. I like Jews.
LEIA: He's Jewish!
BOOPSIE: Really?
D: Yeah. Boopsie, if I draw the star of David on my dick, and you suck it off, you'd be Jewish too.
BOOPSIE: Really? Well, okay.
D: I've got a ball-point pen.
LEIA: I am, at this moment, sticking a cigarette up my vagina.

This night, in the McDonald's parking lot outside of Wrigley Field, my Bat Mitzvah was celebrated. Boopsie O'Flannigan became a Jewess. Leia, in the back seat of the Smith's Camry served as cantor, providing Hebrew music for the event.

We celebrated my spiritual conversion at the bar with beers. Moby, the famous techno artist, was a patron at the dingy Wrigleyville bar that night. I wouldn't go so far as to declare it a most enchanting evening. Certainly, I won't be telling my grandchildren about it. But it was a unique experience.

# 40,000 Feet Above the Earth

## AUGUST 8, 2002 (SOMEWHERE OVER THE ATLANTIC)

I am writing this diary entry from 40,000 feet above the Earth. Our flight from Chicago O'Hare to London Heathrow has been uneventful thus far. Getting to Chicago O'Hare was not.

Mr. Smith realized when we were halfway to the airport he had forgotten the plane tickets at home. The cab had to turn around and drive us back again. Fortunately, Mrs. Smith was one of those freaks who insisted on being three hours early to the airport. We drove halfway to the airport, back to the house, and finally to the airport for real, and we still had time to check-in our bags, pass through security and passport control, and grab sandwiches at the departure gate.

On the plane, Emma is seated to my left. Would she shut her eyes and sleep? She's been a pure joy for the entirety of our journey. Mandy holds claim to an entire row of seats to my left in an attempt to have enough room to stretch out and sleep during the evening.

Our British flight attendants has thick ankles. The British female physique is interesting. Thick ankles, long torsos, thin waists. As an aside, I find British men absolutely hideous. Big ears, long yellow teeth, pale pasty skin oft reddened with the booze. When I see an old Anglo-Saxon man, I often think, Monster! How many people has this old white man screwed over in his lifetime? His children most probably despise and resent him.

Mandy just informed me that she threw away her retainer. Well goddamnit, Mandy!


I pressed the overhead light, which summoned a flight attendant. Several flight attendants banded together to conduct a frantic and surely unpleasant search of the garbage. Lo and behold, the retainer was found in the dinner service's refuse. The flight attendants offered to boil the retainer in water to sterilize the plastic orthodontic device before it was returned to Mandy's mouth. This seemed a call above their duties. We were grateful. However, I was quickly reminded, heat melts plastic. Betty's retainer shrunk in the boiling water and was thereby rendered useless. I knew I was surely going to take the blame for this world-class cock up. I sent Mandy up to first-class to inform her parents of this most unfortunate news. I braced myself for the fury of Hell.

Earlier in the day, on the ride to O'Hare airport I heard Emma say, "Daddy's spotty shirt made him swear." I acted as if I were not paying attention but noted the remark with some spite. No doubt her comment referred to my work in the basement laundry room this weekend.


## WEDNESDAY, TWO DAYS AGO

It was my day off. Mrs. Smith asked if I had done the girls' laundry, and if not, would I. I informed her that I had in fact washed, folded, and returned the girls' clothing to their respective bureaus.

She replied, "great."

Later in the day, Mr. Smith told me I would have to work on a planned day off. I would have to do his laundry. He quickly prattled off the location of his soiled vestments, turned, and left. I retired to my bedroom and called my mother.

"Happy Birthday, Mom. How am I? Well, it's comforting to know I can leave at any time. I haven't signed a contract to be employed here. I'm a free agent."

After all, when I set-up a new bank account in Chicago, I listed my occupation as self-employed. O'Flannigans should not work for other people, my uncle would often say. It is not in our nature to take orders. We're a proud people with a cursed talent for smart-ass remarks.

After hanging up with my mother, I headed down to Mr. Smith's room to collect his laundry. Again, awkward communications seemed to reign in the Smith house.

"Where exactly did you say the laundry was?" I asked softly as I was painfully aware their bedroom was a private space and I felt awkward approaching the threshold.

"The laundry is where it always is," he curtly remarked with a snarky tinge in his Muppet-like voice.

*Dear readers, know that I have never retrieved Mr. Smith's laundry before. Nor have I had the privilege of being treated to a tour of the house's laundry bins.*

I resented Mr. Smith's remark as boorish and I was rather taken aback. I gathered myself and stepped across the threshold of his bedroom door.

Similar to the rest of the house, the parents' bedroom was decorated with a four-post bed, bay windows, and an exceedingly large television. But no laundry basket. The walk-in closet had been converted into a sewing room.

I was pleasantly surprised to learn Mrs. Smith could sew. Who knew she could make herself useful? I saw her present project pinned to a child-sized mannequin - a cute cotton dress presumably for Emma. Who knew! And there I found my quarry - the laundry basket. It contained mostly white items, towels, and tighty whities. I didn't even dare to look for spots, though if I wasn't the one to bear the burden of handling the underwear, I would have found a small pleasure in knowing Mr. Smith sits in his own poo. Also included in the laundry was a blue polo shirt, a pink nightie, and yellow shorts.

I thought to myself, *How much time do I want to spend on the laundry on my day off?* Already resentful, I put all the clothes into the washer as one load. To me, the colored items all looked as though they had been washed many times and were no longer a risk for bleeding. I reasoned, therefore, there was no need to separate the colors and whites. One load would do.

As the washing machine worked through its cycles, I walked to the bank. The walk gave me time to question my decision. I wondered with furrowed brow if the colors would bleed. I prayed. *Please God! Spare me the wrath of Mr. Smith crazed over dyed tighty whities.*

Upon returning to the home, I immediately ran down to the mildewed basement and opened the dryer with anticipatory dread. There was no bleeding! Praise Jesus! No bleeding! However, upon closer inspection, Mr. Smith's blue polo shirt had two small bleach spots. Did I cause those? It couldn't be, I didn't use any bleach. It was pure logic.


## HOUR THREE OF OUR FLIGHT TO BUDAPEST.

Mandy informs me that the destruction of the retainer inspired no great rage from her parents. She has another one she keeps as a spare back home in Chicago. I issue a sigh of relief.

My guru and friend Alice's assignments for my adventure:

-Bring the vibrator
-Read *Jane Eyre*
-Run every day
-Don't be a sasquatch (by which she means, try to be more cosmopolitan)
-Go to the Art Institute of Chicago as much as possible
-Make the most of living in the city

I feel so far, I had made the most of living in the city. I know two ways to drive from the Smith's neighborhood to downtown Chicago.

I can navigate the Elevated train well enough. I've been to a nihilist play and met Moby. I know good parking places in downtown Evanston, and I know how to ride my bicycle to a sandy beach on Lake Michigan.

Alice said I should run every day. I work out regularly in the gym above the boathouse, but I can run more. I should also lay off the coffee. I must stop sneaking cigarettes. The Smiths would no doubt flip-out if they knew I was smoking cigarettes during my breaks. Not that they seem an especially wholesome family, but I think I portray myself to them as wholesome. Why, I declared myself nearly a nun! At least I'm not smoking pot or shooting heroin. My attic room is no opium den. I'm not giving random guys blowjobs. Why not be happy with myself? I should be happy with myself.

It is awkward now around Mr. Smith. I began this endeavor believing he is a great man and he would be my consolation and companion away from Alaska. Over time, my view of Mr. Smith is diminishing.


Mr. and Mrs. Smith summoned me to the dining room last night with a rebuke, "Your quiet manner makes Emma not like to be around you."

To hell with your criticism! That was the moment when the last thread of my optimism was tested. I thought maybe they were expecting someone like the hyper Spanish teacher squawking into the little children's faces.

I defended myself. "I was raised in a little village on the edge of the wilderness. My quiet manner is a sign of deep thought and strong character. Most of today's expected mannerisms toward children are condescending and hyper. Emma doesn't need me to speak in an elevated and high-pitched voice to know that I acknowledge her and am her helper."

*The air remains thick with tension.*

# Hungary



*AUGUST 9, 2002*

The territory of present-day Hungary was occupied in ancient times by the Romans. The Hungarians, or 'Magyars' as they call themselves, migrated from the Black and Caspian Seas in the seventh and ninth centuries A.D. Hungary's first king, Stephen I (997-1038), united the disparate tribes into a country and Christianized it.

During the years of 1867-1918 Budapest, the largest river-port on the Danube, grew from a provincial town into a magnificent European metropolis. Development of the city was centered around a master plan including everything that marked the standards of civilization of that age. The first underground railway in Europe was opened in Budapest in 1896. Hungarian cultural and intellectual life came to rival that of Vienna, and Hungarian society produced some of the greatest scientific minds of the 20th century.

Hungary allied itself with Germany in World War II. At the end of the war the country was under Soviet occupation. The communists established a one-party dictatorship that introduced a reign of terror. With the dissolution of socialism in 1989, the city was again searching for its place among the major European metropolises. In the 2000s, Budapest was reportedly once again becoming a proper Central European capital.

Arriving in Budapest filled me with adventure anxiety. Every sign in the airport was written in Hungarian, or 'Maggy,' the language of the Magyars. It fully dawned on me that I was in a foreign country. Everything was different - the language, culture, customs, manners, gestures. It was my first time overseas. Making some effort, I managed to learn the way to say *thank you* in Hungarian - *Kur Salom*. But faced with the reality of the extreme foreignness of the place, I didn't feel confident in my ability to communicate with Hungarian people. I hope I didn't accidentally offend anyone. Perhaps Ireland would have been a better first foray into foreign travel.

I expected to see Gypsies, or Romas as they are called in Europe. I would very much have liked to see some Gypsies. Filthy heathens outcast by society had always had my sympathy. Jesus hung out with the whores and lepers. Most people had forgotten this detail. I didn't know how I would recognize a Gypsy, though. From what I understood, they had been in Hungary for at least 500 years. In modern times, they are reportedly scapegoats for everything that goes wrong in certain parts of the country. There were reportedly between 125,000 to 250,000 Gypsies in Hungary. My chances of seeing a Gypsy had never been better. Why weren't there any in America? They must've integrated into the so-called great melting-pot like every other immigrant population in America.

The Smith's arranged for a microbus to drive us from the airport to the hotel where we would be lodging. It was drizzling, adding more gray to the somber scenes we passed. Dull and square shanties behind billboards advertising soda and shoes created a strange dichotomy of the remnants of communism hiding behind the flashing promise of capitalism. The microbus hadn't enough room on the road and as it passed oncoming cars I feared we would perish.

The poor Hungarian Gypsies faced not only the dangers of racism but also automobile anarchy.

Mr. Smith used our confinement in the microbus to enlighten us. "It's only been in the last ten years or so since the fall of communism that Hungarians have even been allowed to hear English. English and any aspect of Western culture was forbidden by the Soviets."

*That is interesting*, I thought and anticipated communication troubles therein.

Mr. Smith continued his lecture. "Communism in Hungary is not completely gone, even in 2002. You see, in contrast to other Eastern Bloc countries, where communism was destroyed through popular protests In Hungary, the communist powers here, sensing the changing tide, dismantled the system from the top down. Communism was intentionally downgraded, not violently eliminated. So, in Hungary, sectors of communist power peacefully remain entrenched by design."

Shanties lining the streets became less frequent, the roads broadened, and we were soon in the city proper. The Soviet-style concrete-block buildings gave way to the stunning art nouveau and baroque buildings I had heard of and anticipated. Beautifully hand-wrought iron balconies balanced on stone buildings. I looked up from my suicide seat in awe. Here was the Europe I was expecting.

We settled into our luxury hotel in the heart of the tourist district. I was to share a room on the sixth floor with Emma and Mandy. Mr. and Mrs. Smith had an adjoining suite featuring a small kitchenette and a family room in addition to the lavish bedroom and bath.

The ground and basement floor of the hotel was termed a shopping mall. I wandered it with Mrs. Smith and the girls whilst Mr. Smith napped. The mall was poorly lit, and linoleum tiled, giving it the feeling of an American high-school cafeteria. It served to remind one that communism was not so far in the past. The most notable shop in the mall was a lingerie store hawking frilly and furry wares. There was also a luggage seller and a couple of clothing shops. We bought Mr. Smith a Polo jacket. I wondered if it was a knock-off.

Whilst sipping a cappuccino supplied by a kiosk in the center of the mall, Mrs. Smith said that she, Mr. Smith, and the children would be meeting Mr. Smith's doctor the following afternoon. I

would have that afternoon and evening free. She asked me to go
shopping with the girls in the morning and purchase:

    -Socks for Emma
    -Dish soap
    -Cheese
    -Bread
    -Milk
    -A notebook for Mr. Smith

And lastly, as the forecast called for more rain, I was to find and
acquire three umbrellas. Understanding that one of the three
requested umbrellas was for my use, I appreciated the fact that Mr.
and Mrs. Smith were considerate of my comfort and wellbeing.

# Taking Risks

Dusk set in on our first day in Budapest and the Smiths took me to a restaurant for a family dinner. Mr. Smith was well rested, and everyone's mood was elevated. It was like we were one big happy family. We walked with a mission through the streets outside of the hotel. Mr. and Mrs. Smith had a minor tiff choosing a suitable restaurant. They finally decided on an establishment when both parties acknowledged that the children were absolutely starving. The winning restaurant displayed colored photographs of its most popular dishes on the walls outside the threshold. I was hungry and the food depicted in the photographs appeared adequate. The restaurant was ornately decorated with expensive furniture and fine linens. I choose a dish featuring baked pork.

From ordering to the arrival of the food to our table took over an hour. The children were already jet-lagged and hungry, and waiting so long was rather stressful for all of us. In an earnest effort to comfort the children with distraction, Mrs. Smith put her powder-pink cashmere shawl over her hand and started moving it like a puppet. I was thus formally introduced to "Scarfy," who proceeded to entertain the children and make our wait more bearable. I was impressed with the Scarfy routine. Witnessing Mrs. Smith's creative and fun side increased my respect for her manifold.

I didn't know she had it in her. I made a good joke that they call the country Hungary because the service is so slow.

My much anticipated pork was juicy and tender. We attempted polite conversation between mouthfuls. Mr. Smith asked me a couple political questions and I got the feeling that we didn't have similar views.

"Who did you vote for in this last election?" he probed.

"Ralph Nader," I stated.

"Congratulations," he snorted. "You got George W. Bush elected."

"No, the Supreme Court did that." I was unfazed and the conversation died.

I got the feeling I surprised him by having articulate opinions.

Was the help meant to be dumb? Did I overstep my position by expressing an intelligent opinion?

*O'Flannigans should only work for themselves my uncle would say. The Smiths don't know me. They have invited me to live in their house. They've flown me to Europe and tasked me with raising their children! Discerning readers, I confess, they didn't even ask for references before hiring me.*

*Naturally, I only have raving references to offer. Should they conduct due diligence, they will find no fault with me. I am a responsible, striving individual with a sense for justice and goodness. However, I might feel better if they know a bit more about me as an individual. If they know I've touched other people's lives, that I am trying to make something of my life. Even if they are only to discover that their initial instinctive decision was correct, shouldn't they make an effort to learn more about me? They've entrusted their children to me for fuck sake.*

Halfway through our authentic Hungarian meal, Mr. Smith took a bite of food from Mandy's plate.

Mrs. Smith went berserk. "Why do you always do that?"

"Relax. I only wanted a bite," he squeaked sheepishly trying to avert her wrath.

She did not relent. "I wish you wouldn't do that. What if one of us is sick?"

"I just wanted a taste. I'm not going to get sick," he croaked pleadingly.

Mrs. Smith put down her fork and knife, threw her fine linen napkin on the table, scooped up Scarfy, and stormed out of the restaurant.

I was very uncomfortable. *What should I do? Should I follow her?* Mr. Smith made no move to follow and console her. He let her go and looked down at his plate. *Should I stay with him? Is this sort of scene common in the Smith household?* I stayed with Mr. Smith and the children. The strain saturating the air around us was awkward. We continued to eat and Mr. Smith, seemingly nonplussed, made another attempt at small talk to clear the air.

"I grew up in New York in the 60's."

"Oh," I acknowledged.

"I can remember being able to drive into the city from the suburbs and there being very little traffic."

"Oh." I nodded.

After some moments more of awkward silence, he tried again.

"Have you ever taken a risk?"

*You mean other than going to Eastern Europe with perfect strangers?* I thought. "I've hitchhiked a couple of times in Alaska." *Oops! Methinks that was too much information to confess to someone who trusts me with the upbringing of his children.* It was too late; I'd said it out loud.

"You know that's dangerous?" he said with one eyebrow raised.

"It's risky," I corrected. "I met some interesting people hitchhiking."

Presumably considering himself polite at having given me a chance to speak, Mr. Smith got to the purpose of his question - talking about himself. "I was being treated frostily by my former classmates from my university days. They didn't think I had what it takes to make it big in business. So, I decided to prove a point. Having absolutely no background in the field of computers, I founded a company specializing in the development of artificial intelligence."

"You mean robots?" I attempted to engage.

"The beginning of robots. With hard work and calculated risks, my business was acquired by a New York Stock Exchange-listed firm for a sum in the middle eight figures."

"Oh," I verbalized and nodded. I was prudent enough to know my tit for tat was best kept silent. *Once while hitchhiking, I was picked-up by a guy who later became famous for slashing-up a bunch of school kids with a rusty dagger.*

# All is Commodity



*AUGUST 10, 2002*

**M**rs. Smith alerting Mandy and I there was only thirty minutes left to access the free continental breakfast is what awoke me from my slumber. I was responsible for taking Mandy to breakfast on the second floor of the hotel and staying with her for the first part of the morning. We were meant to collect the items her mother listed the night before at the shopping mall. Little Emma was to stay with her parents. I dressed in haste and only had time to sprinkle on a dusting of make-up, apply deodorant, and throw my hair into a ponytail. I still felt gorgeous.

The offerings at the breakfast buffet were decent. Coffee, tea, cereal, fruit, and pastries- the continental breakfast they called it. I didn't turn my nose at bacon and hash browns, but beggars and choosers.... I poured my coffee, only to discover, with my cup half-full (or empty?), that it would have been best to arrive at the breakfast buffet more than ten minutes before it was to close. I would have to settle for tea. Hot water only trickled from the pot, and I resigned myself to beginning the day without caffeine.

I set out with Mandy to find a store that could fulfill her mother's shopping list. The girls at the front desk of the hotel gave us vague directions in vague English. My situation was rather unlikely if not amusing. A villager from Alaska in an Eastern European city. I was responsible for a young girl and searching rather cluelessly for a grocery store. What were her parents thinking? I was disoriented and scared shitless. *What if we get lost?* My brow was furrowed with tension.

We did get lost. In our wanderings, I located a playground I could take the children to when we have free time. We were found again and, after the morning's journey, I felt a bit more comfortable navigating the streets of Budapest.

The market we located was on a very busy six-lane street. Every product in the store was foreign, but I improvised. Loaves of bread lay piled. Flies buzzed about, landed, washed themselves, then flew again. To be true, I was a bit turned-off. Mandy didn't say anything, so I swallowed my distaste and picked up a loaf.

Then I had to get cheese. The selection was extremely foreign cheese, but I knew brie, so I grabbed a wedge of it. Dish soap was easy to identify. Milk came in cardboard boxes that were heat sealed with foil. It was not fresh milk, but one can put one's faith in heat-sealed foil, I reasoned. Emma was still on the bottle and needed her milk. Surely there was fresh milk in this country, but not in that market.

I hoped the pretentious mother and father of these pretentious children wouldn't get miffed I didn't find fresh milk for their precious baby. Frankly, I too would've preferred fresh milk. But I'd be damned if the market had any. When in Rome... When in a former communist country, the baby would have foil-sealed milk. The notebook I found for Mr. Smith was snazzy. A little spiral-bound notebook with brown and red plaid print on it. Would it serve as Mr. Smith's diary? The young cashier gave me a free diet soda when I checked out. It was my first transaction with Hungarian currency, the Forint, and it was successful.

On the walk back to the hotel, we patronized a fruit stand on the side of a busy six-lane utca - Hungarian for 'street', I learned. I purchased sad grapes, sadder apples, and a few sad bananas. Despite the state of the fruit, I reasoned we were fortunate to have even this bruised, flimsy, and somewhat rotten produce in a formerly communist country. Imagine the times of Khrushchev! Imagine standing in line for hours for cabbage and bread. We had bought semi-fresh fruit from a fruit stand in Budapest. Progress marched on.

In truth, I had always thought of communism as a beautiful theory. I read the Marx and Engles essays when I was a student at college. I was quite sympathetic to a number of their theories. It was true that people could become detached and dissatisfied with their industrial age jobs. I thought it was beautiful to dream of humanity banding together for the good of the whole to create a state where each had his place and each had his needs fulfilled. But waiting hours for a piece of bread? That's a bit much. And here I'd learned the bread was oft swarmed by flies!

Another of Marx's essays proved a bit disturbing to my sensibilities, compounded by the fact that I read it while tripping on LSD. The first line of the essay kept rolling through my mind as waves of intense discomfort crashed upon me, "All is commodity." I read the line over and over. That's an admittedly bleak outlook. Perhaps, however, it could be scientifically proven. All were atoms, electrons, quarks, and whatnot. If these building blocks of the universe could be measured, then they could be counted and possessed. But what about thoughts? Could thoughts be owned? If thoughts were electrical energy passing through a neural network, they could be measured and owned. *All is commodity…. All is commodity…. All is commodity….* Jesus.

My favorite Engles essay was entitled, "On the Origin of Private Property," or something to that effect. In it, Engles proposed that the institution of marriage was initiated by men who wished to know who their own offspring were. They thereby created a system in which they could own the baby maker. Thus, was born the institution of marriage.

I hoped Mrs. Smith would be pleased I bought fruit despite it not being on the list she gave me. As we walked from the fruit stand,

Mandy and I glanced through the window of a pet store. Sweet little newborn mice met our gaze. They were pink but already hearty. Mandy wanted to go in and look and I obliged. The gentlemen at the counter had a bit of an attitude. It's not that he said anything rude. I was taken aback by the fact that he didn't say anything at all. We were not even acknowledged as being present in his establishment. Mandy was pleased by the pet store.

Mandy knew an incredible number of facts about dogs and insisted those in her presence be aware of the wealth of her knowledge. I suspected it was likely she would work with animals in some capacity when she grew up. Though she was young and one's dreams at that age passed like the wind. How many children who said they would be a firefighter when they grow up really did become firefighters? This notwithstanding, Mandy did have a particular attraction to animals and her ability to retain canine facts and trivia was extraordinary. I was sure she could go far with her zoological gift. Her dream of running a Doberman Pinscher kennel when she became an adult may not be too far off. She told me all about her vision for the future in detail. Despite her gift and clear goals, I was doubtful she would materialize the husband named 'Branson'. It was far too specific.

I brought Mandy and our spoils back to the hotel. The brie I bought was rotten. I was sure I perceived Mr. Smith scoff at this discovery. The children would stay with their parents in the afternoon to meet Mr. Smith's doctor. I would have free time to explore the city.

I was careful to remember which streets I walked down and noted where I turned. *Fear of getting lost in this foreign city in which I don't speak the foreign language is undeniable.* I wandered far and aimlessly.

A beautiful outcropping of rock among green hills across from an ornate and massive bridge crossing the Danube caught my eye, imagination, and ponderings. The hill was topped with a giant statue of a beautiful woman in a flowing gown. Holding a book above her head, open to the heavens, she was a woman of knowledge. It was a beautiful and respectful image of womankind. I made a note to be sure to climb this hill during my visit to beautiful Budapest. Not only was the hill topped by a beautiful rendering of a literary woman and a wonderful medieval-looking castle, but it was also the only topography I had seen since leaving Alaska to reside in Chicago. I sat and stared. *This mountain must be climbed.*

Hungry, I stopped by a shop equating to an American convenience store. I purchased cheese potato chips charmingly cut into the shape of the Grateful Dead bears. I also picked-up a pack of cigarettes and a box of matches. *What would the Smiths think if they knew I was smoking?* Fuck it, I was in Europe. After enjoying a smoke or two, I left the pack with what remained of the cigarettes in the window of a haberdasher before I returned to the hotel after dark.

Now, sitting in the lobby of the hotel, I'm writing, dreading returning to my servitude. Oh my God! A couple of hot guys and a pregnant woman just walked into the hotel lobby carrying a television and camera equipment. They are speaking American English. They must be movie makers. I make eye contact and acknowledge them with a nod. I don't recognize them. If they are movie people, they must make B movies. Pornos? I'm hungry again. Grateful Dead potato bears leave one nutritionally wanting.

# Mandy

**M**andy has been aggravating my nerves in a most terrible way. Yes, the "I can't wait until she comes back from equestrian camp" Mandy. The "you make the house more peaceful" Mandy. The "Emma is much easier to handle with you around" Mandy. More recently, she had developed an 'I know everything' attitude and it was not in any way charming.

Today I told Mandy she should live in the present. "You might not even have a future," I added.

Boy, that was a stupid and mean thing to say to a ten year old. I feared the repercussions should that wee slip of my temper get back to Mr. and Mrs. Smith. I could anticipate Mr. Smith red in the face for it. It might even put him over the edge. I already suffered the responsibility for putting bleach spots on his fucking polo shirt. Added to it all, he was there as a witness when I almost fed his children rotten brie. Fuck it. Fuck Mr. Smith, and fuck Mandy's obsession with fucking dogs!

Yesterday I feared I was behaving too contentiously with Mandy. My gruff demeanor was resultant from her righteous know-everything attitude. Traveling with the family and being with Mandy 24 hours a day was causing me to lose my favor for her. I even slept in the same bed as the girl. Did she realize I was paid to spend my time with her? If I wasn't getting cash for putting up with this girl, I'd be rid of her.

In Chicago, before we came to Budapest, Mr. Smith remarked after speaking to the Polish contractors he had hired to paint their house, "Everyone wants to be American." I smiled meekly but thought him vulgarly righteous.

I am reminded of an episode that occurred when I flew to Chicago for the weekend to interview with the Smith family. In retrospect, it was an ill omen and mustn't be ignored nor forgotten.

We were dining together on take-out food as had become usual in the Smith household. It felt awkward to be around them, as had also become usual. The phone rang and shortly thereafter Mr. Smith came into the dining room. He explained with exasperation that a woman had called seeking a background reference for one of his former students. He told her he was eating and that she should call back later. She reportedly "protested," probably assuring him it would only take a minute of his time.

Mr. Smith boasted that he then hung up on the woman! He complained as he sat back down at the dining room table that America was becoming a rude society. How dare the woman! How unacceptably rude to expect him to stop shoving food in his gaping maw for one minute to serve as a character reference for a young graduate seeking employment. He said he would be doing a great favor for the woman by giving her a reference for a potential employee.

*In retrospect, the way I see it, the idiot was doing the kid a favor and he was the one who was unacceptably rude to the woman on the phone. Take a break from lunch, man, and help some kid out. Now I think, if in the future I should ask for a recommendation from Mr. Smith, he will be equally arrogant and rude to my potential employer. Really though, I will probably never use him as a reference because I'm going to get fired. I'm going to get fired for having a breakdown whilst subjected to one of Mandy's dog-obsessed tirades. I'm going to scream at her as I claw at my face, "Shut-up you psychopathic little freak!" I'll be fired as soon as she tells her parents. If her parents are around to witness my psychotic break it will be even more terrible but satisfying.*

MANDY: "Look at the Hungarian Vizsla dog. This breed, the most popular breed in Hungary, was selected for extreme athletic agility, and its skill at pointing and retrieval. Did you know that? I know that because my mental compendium of dog knowledge is vast. All I do is think about dogs, and dogs, and more dogs, and Branson. I bet you didn't know that because no one knows as much about dogs as I do. Anyway, what everyone else thinks they know is wrong. I know so much about dogs that I can't fathom ever learning something new about dogs. Gosh, that makes me a good person."
BOOPSIE: "Shut up, goddamnit!"

I'd say more if I really had reached the limit of my patience with that girl. I'd say such foul things. Things a child should never hear. The consolation in my situation is something Mrs. Smith had said to me on the first day we met - that Emma was better than Mandy. Emma was prettier than Mandy. Emma was already smarter than Mandy (in subjects not pertaining to dogs). Emma will be happier and live a more satisfied life than Mandy. This unavoidable inferiority will certainly eat at Mandy's self-worth for the remainder of her life. That is what I think to myself when Mandy is going on and on about dogs and all I can do to remain composed is zone out.

I have not received any positive feedback from Mr. and Mrs. Smith regarding my job performance. "We're mostly pleased," they managed to muster. If I snapped under Mandy's constant presence, that'd the best I was ever going to hear. For seeking and hiring a nanny over the internet with no references and telling me during the interview weekend that I was perfect, they were lukewarm. Maybe they lost their warmth and idealism when they got married and reality hit. Maybe they lost it when Mr. Smith got a tumor and his cranial "deformity" (as he called it today). Maybe his parents abused him. Maybe they fed him shit brownies. Maybe I should feed them shit brownies.

*This diary could get me in a lot of trouble. More trouble than a discovery of Johnny Rocket, the big silver vibrator.*

# Hare Krishna

*AUGUST 11, 2002*

Dreher 5 is the brand of Hungarian beer I prepare to order as I sit covertly at a cafe and write on my day off. What a day it was, dear readers! More about it later. First, before I burn my fingers with a match lighting a cigarette, allow me to memorialize yesterday's events.

Last night I told Mandy that I was annoyed by her constantly talking about dogs. To soften the blow, I conceded to her that it may be I am envious that she is passionate about something. In all sincerity, I had always considered passionate people blessed. Not everyone on this Earth was lucky enough to find something with which to imbue their life with passion. Apparently, my confession and concession to Mandy went over well. After forgiveness and acceptance, we stayed up into the wee hours talking and giggling. When she finally fell asleep, I tossed and turned all night scheming how I might emigrate a Hare Krishna to the United States.

You see, yesterday walking down Vaci Utca, a pedestrian street lined with tourist shops, I passed a young guy panhandling. He stood out from the crowd as he was dressed in flowing orange robes and a long beaded necklace wrapped around his neck. And he was particularly handsome. Well-formed and clearly healthy, his square-jawed face was glowing with a golden light. I found his shaven head with a wisp of a dirty blonde ponytail atop it, rather punk. I couldn't help but stop and stand right in front of him, my head cocked in curiosity. I'd always had an attraction to misfits and outcasts.

"Hi," I began. "Are you Buddhist?"

"I am Hare Krishna," he softly replied after stuttering.

"Do you live here?"

"Here I collect money," he stated in rather tortured English.

"No, I mean do you live in Budapest? Never mind. Why are you begging?"

In broken English he explained he was collecting money to feed poor women and children. I was glad to hear he was panhandling for a cause. He wasn't a destitute bum. I liked to think he had a warm home, perhaps living in a large apartment with a community of like-minded and orange-robed people. Following Mrs. Smith's advice not to give money to beggars, I didn't give anything to the young Hare Krishna. Mrs. Smith said she would only give female panhandlers money and advised me to do the same. For, said she, "Men can go out and find work as laborers. Women must stay home and care for the children."

I asked the Hare Krishna his name. Silently, he held up a rectangular sheet covered in a layer of peeling plastic lamination. It appeared to be his official Hungarian panhandling license, which listed his name as '*Gabor*'. Zsa Zsa Gabor was Hungarian. Was Gabor his last name? Are Hare Krishnas celibate?


Today I went to the Turkish baths. They were beautiful and decadent. Budapest is famous for its natural hot-spring pools. When the Ottomans invaded Hungary in the 16th century, they constructed the bathhouses around the area's natural thermal springs. Budapest boasts of at least six of these facilities. I visited one located on the other side of the Danube from our hotel.

At one time, Budapest was two cities separated by the Danube -

Buda and Pest. Over time they grew together and now, of course, are called Budapest. Connecting the Buda and Pest sides of the city are several large, beautiful, and ornate iron bridges. The hotel and tourist district are on the Pest side of the river. To reach the baths, I crossed the bridge to the Buda side.

The facade of the Gellert bathhouse was adorned with classical-style marble reliefs featuring scenes of orgies. The interior of the baths were covered with geometrical Turkish tile in art nouveau motifs. I went expecting simply to bathe in a hot spring. We had those in Alaska. Instead, I was treated to European high luxury. Ushered into the women's section of the facility, I gingerly undressed and braced myself as I stepped into the lavish pool room. I understood the Europeans were more free with nudity, and probably nobody even noticed my existence there in the bath. Certainly, no other bather was judging my naked body. It was my first experience with public nudity outside of a locker room, and to be entirely truthful I was mortified.

I discovered massages were available and did not hesitate to secure a session. What is more, the Gellert bath house offered facials, manicures, and pedicures. Alice had told me not to be a sasquatch, which was to say, I should try to be more ladylike. Therefore, I decided to make a point of growing out my leg hair so that I could have it waxed at the bath house on my next visit. Alice would approve.

I finished my stay at the bathhouse with a pedicure for 2,000 Florent, which was about ten dollars.

"I need more nail," the woman complained as she attempted to tame and beautify my Alaskan feet.

She would have understood if she knew the places these gnarled feet have taken me. The pristine beauty of the Alaskan wilderness was accessed through trekking up miles of muddied and frozen footpaths. Freedom, beauty, and a truer perspective awaited those who were willing to traverse those trails. My gnarled feet had brought me through God's country. This was not to say that Alaskan women didn't look after themselves. We were very healthy in a more natural way. Life in Alaska was more about finding inner peace in beautiful settings, rather than seeking a superficial beauty. *All is vanity, Saith the preacher.*

Leaving the baths feeling beautiful, I crossed the exquisite wrought-iron bridge across the Danube. I was back in the tourist sector of Pest. It was high summer and wagons selling ice cream dotted the streets. The Hungarians were seemingly crazy for egg-flavored ice cream. It was a bright yellow concoction that had caught my curiosity.

*Readers will remember a peculiarity with my digestive system wherein ice cream makes me vomit.* I couldn't dare to eat a whole cone of ice cream, lest I vomit up and down the bustling streets of Budapest's tourist sector. Instead, I sidled up to an ice cream wagon and made a big show of looking at each flavor. I was tilting my head on my shoulders and scrunching up my face as if I was trying to decide which flavor to order. I hoped it seemed as if I was having a real predicament deciding which flavor of ice cream I would like. I asked for a sample of the egg-flavored ice cream as if it would help me make up my mind. It was served to me in a small plastic spoon. I was not disappointed. It was strange but good. Remembering my ruse, I pretended I didn't like it. I shook my head at the server and gave a look of displeasure. I tossed away the small sample spoon into a garbage can and walked away.

After satisfying my curiosity about egg-flavored ice cream on a puke-less sized portion, I searched for Gabor the Hare Krishna up and down Vaci Utca. Alas, I could find him not. Then, I took advantage of the Smiths' absence and caught up on my sleep with a sweet nap in the empty hotel room.

---

Now I'm at the cafe and a cold Dreher 5 has been placed on the table for my enjoyment. It's very carbonated. Too carbonated for my taste. A light pilsner, it doesn't have a lot of body or boldness. It's near to mass-produced beers one might drink in America as you head out with your buddies in a pick-up truck to shoot up road signs with a shotgun. But no matter, it'll do. One sip and the world is a little clearer. On the cobble-stoned pedestrian street in front of the cafe where I sit, a gang of teenagers spread out a large cardboard mat. I'm dubious. America is the birthplace of breakdancing, and growing up in the '80s, I've seen some mad shit go down. What do Soviet-raised kids know about breakdancing? But wait! My doubts are shattered when the boombox drops a beat and these boys rip.

Rest, pen, rest. You can caress the pages of this diary later. For now, the beer and breakdancers shall be my comfort in this strange land.

# Fashion

AUGUST 12, 2002

An editorial in an English language expatriate paper I found in a shop on Vaci Utca concerns contemporary Hungarian fashion. Reportedly, after communism shattered, fashion had become an amalgam of cultures, not uniform. Fashion here doesn't have trends. Instead, it was all over the map. Indeed, I saw shops displaying intentionally tattered rags and other establishments purveying pastel old-lady slacks. Commercial establishments like Esprit were represented too. Glorious colorful silks were donned in the streets, and tight jeans had a market.

It struck me as a truism of the new cultural freedom that fashion should not be uniform. Yes, fashion by definition is the prevailing style and custom. But should not one's appearance be a personal statement of the individual? In this sense, fashion would have a central place in a communist society where the importance of the individual was subverted in favor of the importance of the communal. Everyone should dress alike. Why would a free society follow trends? Honestly though, intentionally tattered rags were too much. *It's 2002, people!*

Walking around the city, I'd come to experience Eastern Bloc manners. In shops, the attendants did not smile, with one exception. A young Hungarian lady at a shop selling a Japanese make-up brand smiled, gave me attention, and left me with a positive vibe. She told me I don't need to wear blush with my naturally rosy and healthy skin tone. I have deduced it was improper here to touch unpurchased merchandise. Eye contact from shopkeepers was cold and quickly downcast. I made a resolution to look back. I refused to avert my gaze because of custom. I was told the eyes are the window to the soul and I'm committed to having a spiritual existence. Maybe I come across as a rude American, but I refuse to feel guilty for connecting to my fellow humans from the soul.

In Budapest, I also saw more great butts than I could remember ever seeing. I pondered what is it about this land that produced such fine butts? Meat and paprika? Communistic rations? Good genes? No, I realized - good jeans! In the United States, women had been quite disserved to have found the accepted male fashion to be large jeans fastened mid-crack. Hip-hop fashion was one more way to oppress American women. Enormous jeans pulled down, sometimes below the cheeks, looked positively ridiculous. How was an educated, sensible woman to even consider mating with such a clown.

The baggy jean revolution in contemporary American men's fashion had been paralleled by the low-rise trend in women's fashion wherein one's butt crack was displayed upon sitting. I saw through both trends as another attempt by 'the man' to bring the American woman to her knees. Since at least the Renaissance, the female form had been depicted and displayed as desirable. Illustrated as soft, and receptive, but pure and chaste. Portrayed as objects of male pursuit to be subjected to male desire. Should any gentlemen peruse the pages of this diary he should know this - women have desires too.

Do the oppressive powers of misogyny not understand the best way to bring women to their knees is to have men's asses framed in tight European jeans? Should I inform them? Life would become more enjoyable should American men wear tight-tushy jeans. But I would never aid the misogynist effort. Though I was tempted by the sight of those tight jeans.

My waiter was the ugliest Frenchman I had ever seen. He said he ran the watering hole where I drank in addition to an ice cream wagon down the road. He also claimed to import/export school supplies. He gave me several free beers and, filthy drunk, I stood in the bathroom staring at my face in the mirror trying to find focus. Though an ugly bastard, the waiter was super attentive to me and told me about himself.

After two beers, he also got the lowdown on me. Lying, I told him that I was a teacher. I was ashamed of being a governess. It didn't seem to be respectable work, more like glorified babysitting. I was a college graduate, and I had the debt to prove it. What a situation, to be ashamed to tell a bartender my job. Perhaps he felt the same about himself. A similar feeling of shame could explain why he felt it necessary to mention his importing/exporting gig. He had wild staring eyes, and a balding head round like a volleyball. Large gaps between his small, pointy teeth drew immediate and uncomfortable attention to his sour puss. I had to get the hell out of his establishment.

I stumbled to the Godiva chocolatier in the fanciest hotel in the tourist quadrant. I purchased one piece of all the alcohol-filled chocolates on offer. *Yes, dear readers, I do know how to party.* Then I stumbled into the only Thai restaurant in Budapest to discover most awkwardly that I was the only customer. Window seat? Yes please!

From my table, I had a view over the blue Danube. Being there alone was sad. Why didn't more customers frequent the restaurant? Not only was Thai cuisine the greatest food on Earth - I write this with confidence in my authority - but it beat the living snot out of traditional Hungarian fare. The latter of which was hearty for those who appreciated carnivorous ways, but inarguably bland.

Where did the young people in Budapest party at night? I was sure to find out. What had happened to my waitresses' eyebrows? I would never know. Would I make a friend in Budapest? Would I find the sexy Hare Krishna again?

After eating as hastily as possible, so that I could remove myself from the awkwardness of Thai dining in Hungary, I waltzed to the fountain park to guzzle my fine liqueured chocolates.

I burned my damned fingers lighting my last cigarette.

I didn't want the Smiths to know I smoke. Would they smell it on me? I could tell them people were smoking in the cafe next to me. It was a plausible explanation, as the Hungarian people smoked a lot, everywhere.

---

Now I write in the lobby of our hotel. I have utterly given up on Hungarian nightlife. It is impossible for me to meet people. Is it my shyness? My quiet demeanor formed in the frozen wilderness? My foreignness? Or is it Hungarian society and culture? Most probably it is my shyness.

In the lobby, people come and go, speaking of everyday affairs in French, Spanish, and Hungarian. Japanese too. I would appreciate a Japanese boyfriend. They are clean-cut, quiet, and fastidious. American men are dull. I find Frenchmen are generally fine and suave, though the French waiter today was a slime-ball. What about Hungarian men?

I wonder again if Hare Krishnas are celibate? I doubt it. If I remember the Mahabharata from World Lit. II, Krishna is the lord Shiva in disguise. Shiva, the Phallus King. The lord, ruler, and protector of the phallus. Krishna is the god of dicks. Hare Krishnas most assuredly are not celibate, I reason. In fact, they are most likely privy to high esoteric sex magic.

# Castle Hill

AUGUST 13, 2002

**M**r. Smith was feeling ill after an appointment with his doctor. Mrs. Smith declared she and I would take the girls to the castle district. I was happy to spend some time with Mrs. Smith. We had been getting along well and presumably she would like a break from doctor's appointments, the stress of Mr. Smith's illness, and all things macabre. I was also excited to see the castle. It was my very first castle to see, and a quintessentially European experience to be sure.

Though the castle hill was located only a quick walk across the bridge to the Buda side of the city, Mrs. Smith ordered a taxi to drive us there. It was a tad bourgeois of her, but she had two little girls in tow. I supposed if I had the means, I would be taking taxis around the city as well.

From the riverside at the base of the hill, Mrs. Smith informed us we would have the joy of taking a funicular up to the castle. She had read about it in her guidebook. The funicular, I discovered, was a little train car that traveled on tracks built at a very steep slope. As we ascended, the rickety wooden vehicle jolted sporadically.

Mandy started to hyperventilate. Her mouth was agape and her eyes wide as she frantically searched for balance. I was glad her mother was there with us. I would not have wanted to be responsible for instigating, resolving, nor reporting this classic Mandy episode. Mrs. Smith calmed Mandy in her lap, covering Mandy's head with dear old Scarfy, the powder pink shawl, and whispered soothing sounds at her ear.

All the while, Emma was seated on my lap and stoically taking in the panoramic view of the beautiful city. Emma really was a cool two-year-old. The stark difference between her and her older sister in temperament was laid bare in the funicular.

We reached the top of the hill and Mandy needed both adults to support her out of the funicular as she made a great show of being on solid Earth again. Emma held my hand, appearing nonplussed by the drama. We paused to admire the view. I saw again the huge sculpture on an adjacent hill of a woman holding aloft an open book. I remembered my desire to visit it and voiced my admiration of the sculpture to Mrs. Smith.

"That's not a book," Mrs. Smith clarified. "That's a feather she is holding above her head. It's called Liberty Statue. Much like our Statue of Liberty," Mrs. Smith finished cheerily as a way of softening her clear disdain for my ignorance.

I stood corrected. I could be wrong. Pride was not my sin. Nevertheless, I silently renewed my plan to climb the hill to see the statue up-close. We proceeded to follow Mrs. Smith to our destination.

To be true, I was a little disappointed by my first look at the castle up close. For sure, it was a marvel of beauty and distinctly European architecture not to be found in America. Something I could never see in Alaska. Allow me to explain my initial disappointment. When Mrs. Smith said we would go to the castle, I was expecting a medieval castle. In my imagination I pictured sieges, sovereigns, and sorcerers. However, what I discovered would be better classified as a palace, or an enormous mansion. Grand, indeed, ornate and luxurious to be sure, but not the stuff of fairytales.

It turned out, during World War II, Hitler considered Budapest a red line that the Soviets should not cross. Therefore, the bombing and fighting in the area was heavy and relentless. No place in Budapest was damaged more than the castle hill. To top off everything, the communists finished the destruction as a symbolic expression of their hatred of the monarchy. The castle was rebuilt in more modern times, as the architecture revealed.

We walked around the grounds, admiring the grand gothic-styled buildings. Emma was ever an angel. Mandy needed frequent breaks. As the four of us sat on a bench taking a break, I mentioned my surprise to Mrs. Smith that the castle was rather modern. But of course, I expressed an understanding of the havoc wrought by the communists on such a symbol of the elite. I continued as she nodded and listened. "I despise royalty. I mean, I'm an American." I assumed she could relate. "Just being born doesn't qualify you to be a leader. Being born to have absolute power is scary."

Mrs. Smith nodded while Mandy sniffled miserably with her head in her mother's lap.

I continued. "It is distasteful that a few should be allowed privilege while the many suffer with their basic needs unmet."

"I was born to privilege," Mrs. Smith stated.

"Hmm," I replied. I had thought she had come into wealth upon the success of Mr. Smith's robot business.

Mrs. Smith elucidated, "My family immigrated to America from Poland. We had been landowners and well placed in influential circles. Unfortunately, the Red Army acquired Poland after World War II."

I was stunned and I'm pretty sure my face did not belie my surprise. Was she saying her people were Nazis?

"My grandparents came and did equally well in America. We are a family that succeeds no matter the circumstances."

Now I felt like an ass. I had just been talking about despising the rich and I had been open about my communist sympathies. My audience and employer confessed to being born rich. I shouldn't have been surprised. Should I have been embarrassed? I resolved to not be ashamed of my position. I had always wanted to be a revolutionary, and often, revolutionaries are martyred for their ideals. I would stand firm in my position without embarrassment and without shame.

Thankfully, the conversation was over, and we began our journey back to the hotel. We were more aware of what obstacles we would face as we returned. Mrs. Smith proactively covered Mandy's head with Scarfy as we entered and descended in the funicular. Upon reaching the opposite bank of the Danube, close to our hotel, Mrs. Smith said she would take a distraught Mandy back to the hotel for a nap. I was to take little Emma out for an ice cream.

Emma and I walked the familiar stretch of Vaci Utca in search of an ice cream cart. I saw Gabor, the Hare Krishna. I blushed and looked down as he smiled and attempted to make eye contact. I didn't know why I didn't want to engage with Gabor. I guess I was simply over it. I also wouldn't want precocious Emma to say anything to her parents. I would rather not have my infatuations be a topic of conversation with Mr. and Mrs. Smith. I continued on hand-in-hand with Emma.

As we ate our ice cream on a park bench, Emma said, "Boopsie, do you remember when I was Charlie?"

Shivers went through my body forming goosebumps as I was frozen with knowing. She was talking about a past life, I knew it. I had heard of very young children speaking with uncanny knowledge of lives far away and long ago. "No," I replied to Emma. "I don't remember."

"Boopsie, do you smoke?" Emma asked out of seemingly nowhere again.

"No," I bluntly said, hoping my curt reply ended her line of questioning before it went anywhere even more uncomfortable.

Emma, smart as can be, caught the hint in my tone and dropped the subject.

*I really do have to quit smoking. It is becoming problematic behavior.*

# Evacuation

<AUGUST 14, 2002>

AUGUST 14, 2002

Readers of this diary will not be surprised to learn I am gaining weight on this visit to Hungary. I guess you could say I'm Hungary. Ha! No, 'tis true, in a foreign land one's curiosity compels one to taste all the various temptations as they are completely novel and unknown.

I brought running shoes in my luggage, thinking I would make use of the Hotel's gym. I will tomorrow. I swear. All of my errands are done for the day. When the Smith's allow me free time I will go to the gym and run on the treadmill for 45 minutes. Will they give me free time? When I'm given a full day off, I will also go to the Turkish baths and beautify myself. In one week of working out and eating only salads, I should be back to good form.

I saw Gabor the Hare Krishna today on the street at 5:30. I stopped in front of him and smiled.

"Hello. I have seen you before?" he asked.

"A couple of days ago." Still smiling, I nodded.

"I'm collecting money for food for poor children and families."

"Well," I slyly replied, "I'm going to dinner right now."

"Okay."

"Do you want to come to dinner with me?" I attempted to clarify.

"I don't understand," he said.

"Do you eat?" Again, clarification was needed. Was his low-level of English the problem?

"Yes, I eat," he affirmed.

"With me?" I patiently scaffolded the conversation.

"Me? What with you? I am doing my work."

Gabor the Hare Krishna turned me down. But I tried and maybe gave Gabor something to think about. I struck out, but at least I took a shot.

*A quick note: An elderly Hungarian man just came up to me at the cafe where I am writing, took my hand and kissed it. It was a simple and unexpected gesture. I must be glowing. Was Gabor glowing too? Perhaps the old man liked the look of the stubble on my legs that I'm growing out to have waxed at the Turkish baths. It's like in the old country. Hairy communist women, no?*

I've worked out how I'm going to begin my novel. I plan that when I get back to Chicago I can sit at the computer in my bedroom and begin writing:

A professor once asked me if I believe in unrequited love. 'What a strange question,' thought I. It would seem evident that most love in this world is unrequited.

The novel will follow with first person accounts of unrequited love. Lord knows I have a lot of material.

Gabor didn't get me, nor did he acquire any of my money. Surely most people are put off and uncomfortable when solicited for money in the street. It felt awkward to turn people away, but they see a rich American. They don't see the mountain of student debt. They don't see my ailing mother.

Case in point, as I write these words, a Hungarian man jabbers to me in Maggy- the language of Hungary. He's clearly asking me to give him a Forint. He's neatly dressed, clean, and adequately nourished. Though he does appear to need dental work. All I can do is shake my head and turn my attention to my notebook as I wait for him to quit staring at my hairy legs and wander off.

Gabor is passionate about his 'work'. I suppose Gabor, who begging for the benefit of others, is somehow not as much a pest as others.

*Before enjoying a cappuccino, I'll jot down a bit about the floods.*

The BBC is reporting that the beautiful blue Danube is flooding and the floodwaters have reached Budapest City. It is also reported that the tourist centers are being evacuated as a result. This is either sensationalized spin, or some other tourist center was affected. I haven't heard even a whisper of evacuations on Vaci Utca, the main tourist thoroughfare of Budapest. *I should go back to the hotel to check on the Smith family.*

Upon returning to the hotel, Mandy grabbed me by both arms, her eyes wide with terror. Her manner and the panic on her face alerted me that something was very wrong. *Were we being evacuated from the floods?* Seeking comfort, Mandy told me what had transpired in my absence.

"I was in the hotel spa with Mother," she said woefully. "She sent me downstairs to fetch Papa."

At this point in her tale, I worried something must be wrong with Mr. Smith. And for poor Mandy to be the one to find the ailing man in a compromising condition! *Poor girl.*

"I took the stairwell down, but when I reached our floor, the door in the stairway was locked." She then recounted that she ran up and down the 20 flights of stairs only to discover that all the doors to all the floors of the hotel were locked. Mandy was trapped in the stairwell. She pounded on doors of various floors. Finally, out of desperation, she decided to open the clearly marked emergency exit into the hotel lobby.

"This is an advisable decision," I assured her. "Good for you."

"No!" she exclaimed. "Opening the emergency exit set off the fire alarm. The entire hotel and even everyone in the mall had to be evacuated. It was horrible."

I realized the gravity of her episode. "I see," I said, trying with my tone to de-escalate.

Later, Mrs. Smith told me the hotel security staff had severely scolded Mandy for the incident. "It was bad," she affirmed.

# Punk Nun



Despite my earlier mistake with Mr. Smith's polo shirt acquiring spots of bleach, doing the entire family's laundry has become this governess' regular duty. Was Jane Eyre tasked with the burden of laundry? Methinks a wager to the contrary would prove prudent. But no matter.

I may have shrunk Mrs. Smith's panties in the dryer. They appeared extremely small and inadequate for the job. It might matter if I destroy more of the family's clothing. Perhaps then, I would be stripped of this burden. Perhaps Mrs. Smith's panties are unsubstantial by design.

Presently, I sit at a riverside cafe assessing the rising waters of the Danube, tasting the foam of a cappuccino, and listening to the enchanting one-man band performing on the street. He wears cockles on his stomping feet, a guitar in his honey-hued Hungarian hands, and a Peruvian-like reed flute secured to his neck. He is rather good to look at, and damn can he blow the pipes!

Many street artists are in the tourist district. In addition to the breakdancers I've mentioned before, performers include a violinist with a remarkable blond afro playing on the street, his case open before him, welcoming spare coins for his efforts. Whilst sitting in cafes, diners enjoy serenades by minstrels sporting accordions with an unspoken expectation of payment.

Walking with Mandy and Emma a few days ago, we came upon a man pretending to be a robot. He wore metallic clothing and had painted his face and hands silver. The robot man would stand perfectly still until someone passing by would throw a coin into the tin foil covered cardboard box in front of where he stood. When tipped thusly, he came alive. Keeping his feet in one place he moved in jolts from his joints. Mandy wanted to give the robot man money, so I handed her a forint to pass onto the performer. The robot man patted Mandy on the cheek and she gushed.

I wonder about street performers and Mrs. Smith's advice to not give money to beggars. Did busking fall under this admonition? Were street performers better than beggars? Do they offer a service deserving of compensation? Are they really artists? The one man band at this cafe added to the atmosphere. He was, I suppose you could say, enhancing my experience. I suppose Mandy's life was briefly enriched by her interaction with the robot man. I don't know that it is necessarily transformative and cathartic art. But I conclude that street performance is a more constructive gig than merely flat-out begging. If Mrs. Smith should complain that I gave Mandy money to tithe a beggar, I'd try this argument on her.

Mandy and I regularly talk late into the night in our shared bed. Such conversations smooth over most of our tension and are helped us to bond. Still, having to share a bed with a ten-year-old girl is cramping my self-stimulation regime in a major way. I am horny! Thinking about Professor K—— gives me no relief.

Readers, I did not mail the letter I wrote to Professor K—— when I was in Evanston. He doesn't even know I've moved from Alaska. He doesn't know I live only a few miles down Sheraton Road from him. I am too shy to mail the letter to him. I feel weird about it, a little stalkerish to be honest.


Years ago, as we ate lunch at a Mexican restaurant, Professor K—— told me about a book he was reading. He said the book was focused on the virtue of relinquishing sensual pleasures. The book espoused giving up the pleasures of fine foods, perfumes, luxury, and sex. As he told me about it, I had the impression that Professor K—— was practicing extreme self-discipline as advised by his latest read. I got the impression he was celibate.

But that was more than three years ago. Was it merely a passing phase? Was Professor K—— still a practicing ascetic?

I myself am entirely devoted to spiritual pursuits myself, but in the opposite way from Professor K——- I am a tantric practitioner. My connection with the higher power comes from indulging in the gifts of the sensory world.

I recall a deep conversation I had with a guy who picked me up while I was hitchhiking. He confessed to being an atheist. His confession was one I couldn't understand. When I asked him to explain, he mentioned there is no evidence for the existence of God, and he had no faith.

"But," said I, "everywhere I look I see evidence for the existence of God." I continued appealing to his apparent loyalty to logic, "Creation directly implies a creator."

He nodded, seeming to concede some credit to my reasoning.

New neurological studies show a part of the brain lights up when a human subject thinks about religion. Some scientists cited this phenomenon as evidence for the claim that God is simply a construct of the human brain. That may very well be so. Should it be, I can state the 'God' part of my brain is quite dominant. I'm a spiritual woman. I perceive God everywhere.

Gabor should be enough to fill my fantasies for my remaining time in Hungary. Food for the fires. Why did I look away from Gabor yesterday when I was with Emma? He looked at me with a light of recognition in his eyes and his face seemed to express pleasure at seeing me. Why haven't I told Professor K—— I've moved to Chicago? I think it could be that these things are better left to the imagination. Reality somehow is more messy, chaotic, out of

the fire alarms and causing the inconvenient evacuation of the hotel, Mandy was petrified to leave the hotel, as any such outing required passing by the front desk staff. I managed to coax her with promises of dancing poodles at the circus. As the elevator completed its descent to the hotel lobby and doors pinged open, Mandy hid by slinking at my side. so that, in her mind, she was hidden from the people working at the front desk. To be fair to the child, I did perceive that the desk staff, when they noticed Mandy behind me, gave her an ice-cold evil eye.

With only a little trouble, I found the Opera subway station as Mrs. Smith's sketch directed. Her assertion that the stations were beautiful was accurate. Mandy was pleased to purchase and take responsibility for keeping the train tickets secure and handy. Descending to the platforms, we found well-maintained, white subway tiles lined the walls. Riveted iron columns were painted red and finished with a decorative flourish where they held the low ceilings aloft. What's more, the station was spotlessly clean.

Mandy and I managed to find the proper platform after a couple tries. Boarding the train, dear readers, did cause some anxiety. You see, English is not widely spoken here, and I was responsible for the safety and wellbeing of a child. My body was clenched with stress as I prayed we wouldn't get lost in the foreign city.

"Boopsie, can we get something to eat?" Mandy asked.

Listening intently as each upcoming stop was announced, I told Mandy to stop talking. The metro station Mrs. Smith had directed us to exit at was next. I dragged my charge to the doors well before the train car stopped. As it slowed and came to a jerking halt, we were forced to brace ourselves as inertia slammed us into our fellow passengers. Again, we were the ugly Americans. Apologizing profusely in English, I exaggerated my gestures so that my embarrassment and genuine regret might be clear.

Above ground, I surveyed the scene. We found ourselves in a huge public park with green space, fountains aplenty, and classical sculptures of heroes of the Hungarian state perched atop marble pillars. Mrs. Smith's directions were excellent. I could see the circus in the distance, as it was marked clearly with large signage announcing the location of the 'CIRKUSZ.' The sign was written with colorful illuminated letters affixed to a permanent white auditorium. To be truthful, I was expecting more of a big-top sort of tent affair, anticipating a traveling circus as is custom in America. The Hungarian circus, it turned out, was rather more established with its own plot of real estate.

Unfortunately, we were to discover the circus was closed and no performances were scheduled for that day. Hm, what was I to do? Mr. and Mrs. Smith were expecting me to entertain Mandy until the evening. We had braved the ordeal of traversing the subway and we were in a large park. I figured we could stroll around and enjoy the scenery. Mandy whined at the prospect. I managed to lure her to walk with the promise of an ice cream. Scarcely had our forced stroll begun when we saw signs for a zoo and an amusement park.

Mandy begged to go to the zoo. "Please, Boopsie!" She clasped her hands in front of her as if praying for me to acquiesce.

Now, I knew the girl had a deep and abiding love for animals and, of course, she wanted desperately to visit the zoo. However, I told her we should come to the zoo on another day with Emma. "Won't Emma cry if she found out we had gone to the zoo without her?"

At this point, Mandy was nearly crying, but, I decided, my word is final. I was the governess, after all. "No."

Then I appealed to her ego to smooth things over. "Emma's not big enough for the amusement park. You are the big girl."

Hindsight is 20/20. I knew almost immediately the decision to go to the amusement park was a mistake. We should have gone to the zoo or walked around the park tossing Forints into the fountains for luck.

Faithful readers of this diary will remember my desire to meet a Gypsy. The amusement park was a logical place to make my desire a reality. Before entering the venue, I saw a little woman covered from head to toe in bright and mismatched patterned clothing. She was huddled against a wall, squatting on the pavement. I remembered Mrs. Smith's warning to only give alms to female beggars and, confronted with this poor wretch, I considered her worthy. In good spirits, I placed a large coin at her feet. Imagine my surprise when my charity was to be met with her disdainful screams. The piteous figure she cut belied her strength. She projected the coin with an overhand throw back at me. Her aim true, the coin hit my calf and hurt like hell. This was a bad sign. Gypsy or Carnie, the episode did not bode well for our day.

Mandy was in fact too little for the amusement park. She immensely enjoyed the old-timey carousel with beautifully painted horses which slowly moved up and down as the ride rotated to merry music. However, a proper rollercoaster proved to be too much for the little girl.

You see, I managed to convince Mandy to go on a water-ride roller coaster through sustained, friendly encouragement and some cajoling. It had a child friendly appearance, with box cars painted with cartoonish animals. The August heat also helped in convincing her it would be a refreshing experience. We sat together in a car adorned with a purple walrus flashing a toothy grin. The gayly painted ride was deceptive. Should one be surprised that roller-coasters in the Eastern Bloc didn't face the same requirements to adhere to safety standards as ones in the West? The ride did not feature seatbelts. And it was fast and furious.

Mandy puked and cried. Both of us were splattered with vomit. When it finally finished and we were freed from the ride, I guided Mandy to a bench and tried to hold her in my arms.

"I'm so sorry, Mandy!" I repeated over and over. I knew the report of this event would not go over well with her parents.

An older man was sitting next to us. Dapper in a cheap gray suit and mustachioed, he resembled Albert Einstein a bit. He caught on to our distress. Perhaps her tears, or my attempt at comforting her gave away our predicament. Perhaps it was the reek of the splattered vomit. He made eye contact with Mandy and gave her an animated smile as he bounced around with exaggerated silliness in a sweet attempt to comfort her. Mandy's sobbing abated and she sniffled.

Sincerely appreciative of this stranger's kindness, I could have hugged him. I tried to thank him in English, but it became immediately clear he didn't speak any. He winked at me, a universal gesture let me know he understood the sentiment nonetheless. I smiled at him kindly.

We sat quietly together for a few minutes. A scantily clad but heavily made-up woman approached the gentleman. With the universal gesture of shimmying her big boobies at him, she appeared to publicly proposition him. The woman pushed her voluptuous chest into his face as she whispered something into his ear. He tipped his hat to me and walked away with the minx. I stared aghast at what had just occurred. I couldn't believe it.


That, dear readers, was how it came to pass that I, vulnerable and stunned, found it necessary to explain to a ten-year-old what a prostitute is.

# Deluge



I must write all about Ole, The Norwegian Oil executive. But first, dear readers, I can report that the monsoon storm predicted for the muggy heat of August came to pass. I was out walking aimlessly and watching the world in wide-eyed wonder when it happened.

I had, moments before, departed from a cafe along the shores of the Danube where I had enjoyed a quite-decent cappuccino. When, in an instant, the color of the sky changed and darkened. What followed was a fast and violent downpour such as I have never experienced in Alaska. In Alaska, the rain was more of a mist which continued unabated for weeks, serving to soak one through to the bone. This was something different altogether.

The admittedly impressive thunder and lightning was not as remarkable as was the sheer volume of water that fell with no warning. These weren't raindrops, this was a deluge.

Seeking shelter at Anna's, a famous bar in the tourist sector of Budapest, I soon became forlorn. There were many others dodging the deluge in the bar, and thusly packed, I couldn't command the bartender's attention without shouting in Hungarian. I nudged myself slowly, step-by-step through the crowd up to the bar. Next to me on red-cushioned stools sat several Hungarian women. I waited and waited, between their puffs of Davidoff cigarettes and hairspray, to be tended to by the bar staff. Rudely, quite intentionally rudely, I was ignored by the service.

It must have been because, with my discreet make-up and modest dress of basic American jeans, I did not fit in with the desired clientele. Which appeared to be local Hungarian women dressed in tight mini-dresses. Their garments were designed with cut-outs placed in rather revealing places on their bodies. If I had similarly plastered-on bright and conspicuous make-up and sprayed my hair up, perhaps I too, could have been served a beer at Anna's.

Standing at the other end of the bar with his elbow resting on the marble top was a handsome and suave looking swain in white pants. He was grown but young, his mid-thirties. Old enough. Judging by the white slacks he wore, and his smooth olive skin and curly brown hair, he appeared to be Italian. From his gaze, I knew he was interested in me, but I felt awkward and only looked at the handsome patron in his lusty brown eyes. Growing angrier from being ignored by the waitstaff, I gave the swarthy Italian a look of disgust and said, "What?"

Hearing myself through European ears, I profoundly and fully understood why Americans have a reputation of being 'ugly.' My utterance came out as more of a, "Whaa?" To the suave and cultured Italian, it was undoubtedly crass and uncouth. But forget friends, I needed a beer!

Defeated, I gave up on ever being served. When the monsoon-like downpour had abated enough, I moved to the Frenchman's street-side beer-stand. There I had become something of a regular. Located a few hundred meters from our hotel, the establishment was plain and basic, with only a few white plastic tables with chairs around. But there I knew I would be served. The only problem there was that I risked being seen by the Smith family should they venture out.

Faithful readers will remember the terribly unattractive French waiter here. I learned his name was Francois. I purchased two pilsners, and as before, Francois gave me the third gratis. Truly,

Francois was not much to look at. He destroyed the stereotype of the handsome and debonair Frenchman. His head is the shape of a basketball, and his buzz-cut thinning hair did nothing to flatter the globe. Francois' fatal flaw though was his teeth. They were not the typically bad yellow and browning European teeth. Instead, they were very small with gaping space in between each little ivory pin. Francois sat in an empty chair beside me and talked with me from time to time. But business was booming with tourists and locals alike escaping the rain. Francois and I could barely finish a thought let alone hold a proper conversation before he had another glass to refill.

I sat in a plastic picnic chair and waited for Francois to be free to converse with me. When he did have a free moment, he sat in a free chair beside me and asked if I had made any friends in Budapest. I told him I had met Gabor the Hare Krishna. Francois called Hare Krishnas crazy. Was he right? To me the Hare Krishnas simply seemed to be deeply spiritual people. In this day and age dominated by blatant materialism, to express your spirituality outwardly was considered crazy. Francois excused himself from my icy reception to tend to his other customers. I grew tired and left my beer for a bathroom break.

The bathroom of Francois' establishment was housed in a building behind the open air beer stand. I deduced that Francois lived upstairs in the same building. When I returned from the bathroom, I discovered the chair Francois kept open beside mine to sit in when he could take a minute's break had been sacrificed to another patron. I reasoned Francois didn't have time to pay me the attention I sought so I left his shit hole.

I walked up and down the wet streets of the tourist sector and wandered into a tunnel serving as a pedestrian walkway under a road. There I witnessed three apish men teasing an elderly Roma beggar. The beggar sat unmoving with his legs outstretched and his back propped against the wall of the tunnel as the three men laughed and taunted him. Judging by the behavior of the monkeyish men, they were Americans. Most likely American frat boys.

The stereotype of ugly Americans would seem to be well deserved. I would not take it upon myself to apologize for my countrymen. However, I would freely admit my own failings and ask our European cousins for grace.

I watched the obnoxious Americans as they dismissively tossed the beggar a coin. The coin missed the beggar's small plastic cup and rolled to a stop at my feet. I picked up the coin and placed it politely into the old man's cup. This is the moment when I met Ole. Having witnessed the whole scene as it unfolded in the tunnel, Ole came up from behind me and silently took my arm. Surprisingly unalarmed at having been accosted by a stranger, I looked at him questioningly. He was tall, fair, and attractive. He emitted an especially kind countenance. The stranger smiled down at me gallantly and asked if I would join him for the evening.

# Grand Prix

Accompanied by Ole and his friends, I suddenly found myself an honored patron at Anna's, the trendy bar where just earlier the same night I had been blatantly ignored. Ole managed to secure seating for us at a big wrought-iron table in the garden behind the bar front. He ordered a bottle of red wine, and it came promptly with no delay nor snobbery from the wait staff.

Ole was attractive. Tall and solidly built, he did sport extra weight in his mid-section, as is considered typical for men his age. His hair was dark blond and thinning, but it still covered, however sparingly, both the perimeter and the expanse of a normal hairline. His eyes were a piercing light blue that twinkled perceptibly when he smiled. Ole's most notable physical feature was that he had only one arm. His left arm was missing from the bottom of the shoulder down.

When we were seated, Ole introduced me to each of his friends. They were a Formula 1 racing pit-crew from Norway. It just so happened that the Hungarian Grand Prix was a very big deal in European motorsports. Ole was an executive for a big oil company that had operations extracting gas from beneath the Norwegian Sea. As was standard for big oil companies, they sponsored contenders in the Hungarian Grand Prix. Ole had accompanied the company's crew here in Budapest for the big race scheduled for tomorrow. It's a perk of his job he boasted with a cute grin.

Lubricated by frequently refreshed bottles of red wine, we passed a beautiful night together. The pit-crew were good, hard-working people. 'Salt of the Earth,' my uncle would say. Most of the boys I grew up with in my village were motorheads. They're my kind of people and I felt comfortable in their presence. The lead mechanic, Jan, and I got along especially well. Seated in the chair to my right, Jan was a father of three young girls back in Norway. He was clearly comfortable in the company of younger females, and I was especially at ease with him.

"O'Flannigan? You must be Italian?" Jan joked.

"No. You're thinking of my cousins, the DeFlannigans," I quipped.

Seemingly jealous of my conversation with Jan and wanting all of my attention to himself, Ole inched his chair closer to mine. Gently but decisively, he took my hand in his right and only hand. He studied me to gauge my reaction. When he apparently approved of my level of comfort with his touch he looked intensely in my eyes.

"Boopsie, your energy is beautiful." He confessed, "You are the second-most beautiful woman I have ever seen."

"Only the second?" I questioned while consciously animating my face to express both disbelief and disappointment.

The pit-crew laughed at my antic, which was precisely the reaction I had been aiming for. It was a lively and jovial evening. I was glad these gentlemen appreciated my humor.

Ole, however, didn't relent. "The first most beautiful woman was in Brazil."

Uncomfortable with the course the conversation was taking, I changed the subject. "So, Ole, if you don't mind me asking, how did you lose your arm?"

The entire table hushed, and everyone turned their attention to Ole's answer. It turns out Ole lost his arm in America. He had been on holiday in Florida with his wife and children. Water skiing was fun until it wasn't. Ole lost his hold of the tow rope and spilled into the water. Another boat ran into him, and the boat's rudder did the dirty work. The surgeons did what they could.

When Ole had finished telling his story to a rapt audience, I attempted to break the awkward silence that followed. Turning to Jan I asked, "So who do you think will win the Grand Prix tomorrow?"


After many drinks and much laughter, Ole and I parted ways with his company and walked arm in good arm for a stroll down Vaci Utca. Passing Francois' establishment, I saw him, and we made eye contact. I did not, however, acknowledge him.

Ole and I stopped our ambulation by a public fountain. The fountain was designed perfectly for sitting on. Four identical lions sat in a sphinx-like pose. Each lion was situated 90 degrees from the last so that one lion was facing what presumably was each cardinal direction. Between each beast were large stones intended to serve as benches. Water was ejected from the mouth of each lion into stone basins underneath.

*However, readers, it is not my aesthetic interest in the sculptural aspects of the fountain which drives me to recount this scene. What transpired on the sitting stones between the lions is what is of particular interest in this scene.*

Sitting together on the stones aside the fountain, Ole told me of his troubles. Ole, it would seem, was not happy with his life in Norway. You see, it was not easy to keep up with his wife's unending demands for material comfort. One must have a house, "Because," he stated, "renters are nobodies." Adding to a homeowner's nearly unbearable woes, said house must have a sauna, several bedrooms, underfloor heating, vaulted ceilings, granite countertops, and garage space for every family member's car.

"Life is so hard," Ole concluded.

Now readers, by now you know me well enough to ascertain that I didn't feel any pity for Ole. He had been very kind to me. He was by any measure a likable guy. Nevertheless, to me these weren't relatable as actual problems. He'd become yet another upper-class white guy complaining about keeping a wife.

Having dumped his emotional burden, Ole became frisky. He

put his single hand on the back of my waist, pulled me in close and kissed me. I relented to Ole's affections. Strangely, when he felt me up, he rubbed the back of his hand on my breast. Was this learned behavior? Was this cultural? In my experience, American guys groped a woman's breast with the palm and pads of their fingers. Maybe Ole used the back of his hand because he only had one hand, and had developed super-sensory powers to compensate for the lack? Perhaps the palms and finger pads of Ole's one hand were too sensitive to touch my pert teets?

Giving his tongue a break from probing the depths of my mouth, Ole promised me tickets to the Grand Prix on Sunday… if I agreed to sleep with him. This was one step too far.

"Ciao!" I stood up abruptly and left Ole in the darkness sitting beside the lion fountain.


I didn't dart-off because the subject of sex being raised insulted my modest sensibilities. No. I found it insulting that his offer for Grand Prix tickets was predicated on the condition of my having sex with him. If Ole had offered me sex, but not tickets, would I have slept with him? There's a chance.

Am I truly the second-most beautiful woman Ole has ever seen? I can smell Ole on me as I write this diary entry. He was kind to me. I found him to be a fine Norwegian, indeed. But Ole is married with children. Admittedly, he has big marriage problems. And the poor thing has huge loans on his house, sauna, and four-car garage. Will I call Ole for tickets to the Grand Prix? Probably.

# $\mathcal{P}$ en $\mathcal{G}$ ames

AUGUST 17, 2002

nother day, another café. I have run this pen nearly dry. After last night's frightful storm, Budapest is hot and humid. and the wind blows wildly. I must write Alice a postcard telling her of my romp with Ole. Will I call Ole and see him again? I will talk with Mrs. Smith to ask for time off to attend the Hungarian Grand Prix today. Alas, I think it may be too late. Why didn't I go with Ole to his hotel? I find him very attractive. His marriage was inconsequential. In Europe, marriage in general seems inconsequential.

I walked to the fountain park where late last night Ole and I made out. There was a wedding party sending off the bride and groom to what was sure to be a life of resentment and regret. The horn of the newlywed's hot rod played the '*Tequila*' song. Classy.

Walking alone gave me time to think. I was, framed by our impending departure, reflecting on my time in Hungary and my impressions of the country. My thoughts were that Hungary was very nice. However, I would never want to live there. There must be better places than this, surely. I missed Chicago. I wondered what Leia was up to. I hoped she had found a job.

What was Professor K—— doing now? Why didn't I send the letter telling him I've moved back to Chicago? I had confessed my love to him last year via email on 9/11. I reasoned that if the world was going to blow up, erupt into total chaos, or at least descend into World War III, I had better confess outright my love. My email to him didn't mention the children or white picket fence of my imaginings, I simply wrote I may be in love with him. That may have been the moment things became hopeless for me and Professor K——.

---

This pen has drawn a mark most accidentally on the fine tablecloth laid out before me. I shall hide the mark under a napkin, pay for my meal, and run away so as not to admit responsibility for staining it. As has frequently been the case in my adventures, I am the only patron at the café.

Because the pen has become a topic, I will make a confession, dear readers. Diaries are a safe place to confess. A private way to get something off one's chest. A way to lighten the load of the human consciousness in secrecy. I confess, I have been playing a little game on Mr. Smith.

You see, Mr. Smith kept a diary too. From time to time, I have been stealing Mr. Smith's pens. The pen game is played slowly, methodically, and with patience. At home in Chicago, Mr. Smith kept a big cup of various writing utensils on the desk of his home office. I took one at a time whenever I found myself alone in the house. Whilst traveling, it was whenever the opportunity arose. I leave them in random places - a cafe table, a park bench, or on a seat of the cogwheel trolley that traversed up and down the bank of the Danube unchanged since 1973.

I made sure Mr. Smith noticed me using different pens to write in my own diary. Pens that are uniquely mine. From time to time, he has asked to borrow my pen, as he couldn't locate his own.

"Where are they?" I've heard Mr. Smith wail through the cracked door connecting our hotel rooms.

Now that this pen has neared the end of its usefulness, I will purchase a new pen from a street vendor. Slyly but nonchalantly, I'll be sure Mr. Smith notices my new pen which is nothing like any of his missing pens.

The pen game is not a mean-spirited game, gentle readers. I simply need some outlet for dealing with the way he makes me feel. The man is so rude and condescending. I'm an intelligent woman. Maybe not so poised, and admittedly not shrewd, but I am intelligent. Mr. Smith talks to me like I am an idiot. He treats me like I am in the way, when in fact, I am raising his fucking children. The children he is not capable of caring for without the paid help of strangers. So, you see, the pen game is a silent and harmless way of venting.

This morning I went to the gym and did a couple cycles of using sauna followed by a plunge in the cold tub. I read of the benefits of the hot-cold immersion cycle and thought it might help detoxify from my night of red wine and heavy one-armed petting.

Our hotel had a beautiful and well-equipped gym. However, I did not bring my swimsuit on my travels to Hungary and was thus naked as I went through the detoxifying routine. It was normal to be naked at the Turkish baths in Budapest. The men and women were also segregated at the Turkish baths. The hotel gym was not segregated. I wasn't sure of the tolerance level for nudity in the hotel as it was mainly occupied by foreign guests with differing sensibilities. Granted, I was alone in the facility. However a window from the weight-room overlooked the cold tub. Should some other health-conscious hotel patron decide to pump some iron on their holiday, the entirety of my flesh would be on unfortunate display. It was exciting to be publicly naked.

As I switched from one extreme temperature to the next, I felt my blood pumping and the oxygen flooding into my veins. The risk inherent in public nudity surely contributed to the adrenaline flow.

# Brothers



AUGUST 18, 2002

I've acquired a new pen, and I have become a new woman. Truly, I do feel irreparably changed by the events which transpired last night.

After my responsibilities with the Smith family had finished for the evening, I escaped to Vaci Utca. Once again, seeking easily found anonymity. I was motioned-to invitingly by two men sitting at a bistro. Hesitantly, but with a spirit of adventure, I agreed to join them at their table. They were Germans, brothers in town for the Grand Prix.

The men showed me pictures of the race on the small view-screen on the back of their digital camera.

"Is that your wife?" I asked one of the older gentlemen as I paused scrolling through photos and pointed at a chubby figure in a picture.

"That is me," he said.

"Oh." I winced perceptibly at my faux pas. Staring down at the table, I tried to speak away my shame, "The picture is so small… It's not clear."

Otto, the older of the brothers whose company I was delighted to share, was an artist, an antique appraiser, and a master flutist. He was quite a bit heavy, but handsome with wavy blonde hair, and bright blue eyes. Roman, the youngest of the brothers, claimed to be the most respected management consultant in Europe. Roman was extraordinarily handsome. Young, slight, and dark, I found myself highly attracted to him.

Over dinner, Otto reminisced fondly about his boyhood in American-occupied Germany during the reformation. Roman was ten years younger than he and hadn't been born yet. Their father had been a landlord for apartment buildings in which American soldiers were housed. Young Otto would deliver papers to the tenants of his father's buildings. He recalled the American soldiers being friendly and kind to him. This early experience made an impression on him and he maintained a high opinion of Americans throughout his life.

"What do you think of George Bush?" Otto asked me.

"I'm embarrassed to be American because of him. George Bush is a complete idiot, and it scares me that he's the most powerful man in the world. He's a Nazi," I concluded.

Roman raised one eyebrow. "A Nazi?" he asked quizzically.

"George W. Bush's grandfather managed a bank that moved funds for financing the Nazis. He founded the family dynasty on the profits from the venture."

"I didn't know that," said Roman.

"He is a puppet to a mad regime," Otto stated. "Germans believe he is mad."

It came as little surprise to me the German perspective of American current affairs was that George Bush was a mad marionette. "He would be a good man to have a beer with," Otto said, "but a bad man to run the most powerful country in the world."

The brothers paid for my excellent chicken dinner and convinced me to go out with them so that we could continue our pleasant evening at a bar. With the top down in Otto's silver BMW convertible, we raced through the streets of Budapest. A CD played

Vivaldi loudly out of the car's speakers. Roman explained the music was Otto's performance with the German National Orchestra. I was impressed. We drove to Beckett's, an Irish Pub. There, the brothers and I danced with carefree exuberance to a cover band playing American songs from the late 1970s and early '80s. I drank plenty of Guinness and the brothers got the tab.

The three of us walked back to Roman's beautiful apartment across from the American Consulate. His apartment was sparsely furnished with a couple of beat-up leather sofas on the bare parquet floors. No curtains were hung above the grand neoclassical windows. We switched from drinking beer to hard alcohol.

We decided to take a photo to memorialize our beautiful night together. We spent some time drunkenly fiddling with Otto's camera, trying to figure out how to set the timer so that we could take a photo of all three of us together. For the photo, we sat together on one sofa, me in the middle with my arms around each brother to either side.

The brothers asked if they could take pictures of my tattoo. I agreed. Wearing a cropped shirt and denim pencil skirt, it was easy to modestly lift my shirt a bit in the back so that they could view it closely.

*Yes, gentle readers, On the small of my back is a tattoo of a puffin, the Alaskan marine bird, smoking a cigarette. In retrospect, it's clear it was a bad decision to get a tattoo, but I've seen stupider tattoos.*

Otto broke out his golden flute and played a moving solo. He was truly a talented man and I had never seen a golden flute before. Again, I was impressed. Otto was clearly a master of the instrument. Despite my own aptitude with the instrument, I declined an invitation to follow his performance, sure of my humiliation.

Musical performances finished, the question-game ensued. In the question game, you could ask any player any question and they had to answer truthfully. There could be no judgment in the question game, only earnest interest.


*The Question Game:*

BOOPSIE: What is the strangest thing you have done?

ROMAN: I was with a woman who liked me to tie her up and spank her with a whip.

OTTO: I was with a lawyer who wanted me to go out on my balcony and give a speech like Hitler while she gave me a blowjob. It was the only way she could have an orgasm. A neighbor came to me later and asked me if I had heard someone giving a speech like Hitler. I said yes, I had heard someone giving a speech, but I had not heard 'Heil Hitler.' I had heard 'Ein liter!'

ROMAN: What do you want to do to us?

BOOPSIE: I will bite Otto's ass while I give you a hand job.

ROMAN: What more do you want?

BOOPSIE: I want to take a shower. I'm on my period.

OTTO: We love your blood, honey.


The three of us drank more and it was decided that I would start with Otto and then go do Roman. Otto and I undressed. He had a huge belly. His physique reminded of the honey-bear squeeze bottles. I had never been with someone as old as Otto. He did it missionary style. His weight crushed me, and I could hardly breathe underneath him. Truth be told, readers, should any moans have escaped that room last night, they were due to want of oxygen. I survived the ordeal, and we cuddled before I went to Roman for more.


*The brothers are not circumcised. It's the first time I've ever been with an uncircumcised man. A vast majority of American men are circumcised. I have read that soldiers were circumcised for hygienic reasons before being assigned to the trenches in World Wars I and II. When the soldiers returned to America and procreated, they chose to have their boys circumcised as they had been. I am from here on convinced to not circumcise any male children I may have. What a terrible idea circumcision is! Taking a highly sensate developing being and slicing off a chunk of its most sensitive body part. This is not optimal for the baby's development, methinks.*

I asked Roman more about the woman he tied up. He confessed she was an intern at his business. He would tie her up, leave a vibrator inserted inside of her, and leave her like so as he went grocery shopping. I inquired about a woman who had called while we were at the Irish Pub. Otto had called her Roman's girlfriend. Roman hadn't much to say about her. I asked him to tell me about the women he has loved. He said he loved a woman who was a dancer. I ask him for his thoughts on unrequited love. Research for my novel, you see. He said he knew it existed, but one couldn't dwell on these things.

Whilst kissing, I noticed Roman's tongue was forked- it was split about a half of an inch right down the middle. I had heard about body modification freaks in the US who cut their tongues to make them forked. I asked Roman about his anatomical oddity. He swore to me he was born with his tongue forked. I became unnerved and got out of his bed and dressed quickly trying not to reveal my discomfort. It was not lost on me the irony that after the absurd intimacy I'd had moments ago with both brothers, the strange detail of Roman's tongue was what gave me discomfort.

I gathered my things and left my email address scrawled on a scrap of paper torn from this diary. I suggested to the brothers that we meet again someday in Cuba. My suggestion was met with warm agreement and a group hug. I took my leave and hiked back to the hotel. The streets of Budapest were empty at that late hour. I slipped into bed with Mandy.

As I lay in bed, I replayed in my mind the night's highlights. My thoughts always returned with a jolt to my discovery that Roman had a forked tongue. He claimed to have been born with it and Otto confirmed his assertion. Had I then met Mephistopheles?

# Dear Alice

<br>

D*ear Alice,*

*Please find herein a brief retelling of my last few days in Hungary. Our time here is coming to a close, and I would like to relate certain adventures for your enjoyment. Please feel free to fill in any gaps you may find with your imagination.*

*I decided not to go with a one-armed oil executive to the Grand Prix. Instead, I wandered far, trying to avoid the tourist sections of town. I met two men. They were Germans, Otto and Roman; 50 and 40, respectively; Brothers. They bought me dinner and drinks. We retired to Roman's central Budapest apartment. More drinks of hard liquor followed. We were treated to a flute solo from Otto, who played a golden flute.*

*Later we played the question game. I restrained my urge to ask any bestiality questions, for fear they wouldn't know I was being facetious - a feat of great will. 'Twas very much fun. They helped me decide that I will not circumcise my future sons. We agreed to meet again in Cuba.*

*The next day, I took the Smith girls to the zoo. Before going, I grappled with a moral question. Is the suffering endured by the individual animal caged and gawked at in the zoo worth the benefit? Mrs. Smith answered immediately and nonplussed, as if the question didn't even deserve a moment of contemplation. In Mrs. Smith's imperious opinion, zoos are assuredly justified in imprisoning inno-*

cent animals. I told Mr. and Mrs. Smith about the time I rode my bike out onto the tundra in the middle of the night on a mission to free two caged reindeer. The mission was aborted as I ended up making out with an East Coast guy. Mr. Smith made a snide comment, "Sorta like Free Willy."

At the zoo, among the wonderful and exotic things I beheld was a datura plant. I knew about datura from the botanical writings of Terrance McKenna. The plant's large trumpet shaped powdery orange flowers are unmistakable.

This was the hallucinogenic plant that is inserted vaginally with a dildo-like object. Used thusly, datura gave rise to the legends of witches riding their broomsticks through the skies. I took some leaves from the datura plant from the zoo intending to make a poultice for my own experimentation. Despite its public location, it was not hard to discreetly remove leaves from the plant, as the zoo was bustling with families, school trips, and gypsies. Those monkeys sure drew a crowd with their antics too! I placed the datura leaves in a cigarette pack in my purse for safe keeping.

The next day I went to a park where many of Budapest's homeless people stay. It served as my sanctuary in this strange land. At the park I seek and find solitude. There I knew I wouldn't see the Smith family and I could enjoy smoking cigarettes at my leisure. On this day, I smoked a cigarette or two, and returned home to make the hallucinogenic poultice in the hotel bathroom.

Horrified, I discovered that I had left the datura in the pack of cigarettes in the park.

Now I am frightfully paranoid that a homeless person has found the bag and associated the datura in the cigarette packaging as leaves for smoking. Datura is poisonous – very highly poisonous if ingested improperly. What if a homeless person salvaged my cigarettes and, curious about the plant matter in the bottom of the box, assumed it was a smokable leaf?

Visions of the poor poisoned urchin being sent to the emergency room in a hospital for the impoverished have hijacked my imagination. The doctors discover he has been poisoned. The police are notified and in their investigation they learn from witness descriptions that a young woman in a red dress with glasses had been seen frequenting the area. Police alerts are issued throughout the city: Be on the lookout for a bespectacled woman who poisoned a vagrant.

I can't let myself be seen in that park again. I'm so scared that I have killed a poor homeless Hungarian. What if they fingerprint the cigarette package? Christ! Pray for me, Alice.

Reporting on your instructions to not be a sasquatch, I am doing what I can *to be more cosmopolitan and ladylike. I went to the thermal spa and had my armpits, bikini line, and legs waxed. Truthfully, it was terribly painful. All of my hair follicles are bright red. I must look diseased.*

*I'm very ready to return to America. I miss Alaska. I miss you and your dogs. Do they think I've abandoned them? Do they miss me?*

*Leia's boyfriend wants to hook me up with his friend, an actor/medical researcher. I might go for the action. But considering that there are quite a many-million men in Chicago, how could I possibly give my attentions to only one?*

*The mother I work for, Mrs. Smith, is not so bad. More than tolerable. Things are awkward with the father. I'm going to kill the ten-year-old. She is a little know-it-all who is fucking obsessed with dogs. I'm going to fucking kill her. You'll see me on CNN under the headline "The Crazed Nanny." I'm at the end of my patience with that girl.*

*I hope you are doing well and enjoying your last few days of summer. I'll be sure to write to you a new updates upon my return to America.*

*I Miss and Love You,*

*Boopsie*

# Hollywood



AUGUST 19, 2002

In the hotel lobby I sat slouched in a plush armchair as I dreaded the eventual necessity of returning to the bed I found myself sharing with a ten year old. Fortunately, our time in Budapest was drawing nearer to a close. We are to fly back to Chicago the day after tomorrow. Across the room, I spotted a man and a woman sitting seemingly radiating contentment in each other's company. I recognized them from our first full day in Budapest as they were loading filming equipment into the elevator.

The man was trim and tall with tanned skin, and his wavy hair had a tint of sun-kissed yellow. The woman's long brown hair was similarly sun-kissed and tied-up in a tight ponytail. She was lanky and fit, though one couldn't help but notice she was heavily pregnant. She was stunningly beautiful and emanated an Earth-mother vibe. I was intrigued by the couple from the moment I saw them. Now would be a perfect chance to talk to them and find out what they are doing in Budapest.

Naturally a reserved and shy person, it was unusual for me to approach strangers. However, there was something magnetic about these two and I wanted to know them. I did feel a bit awkward when I delivered my opening line, "Hi. I'm Boopsie." Smiling in the hope it might make me come across as less of a freak, I went for it. "What brings you to Budapest?"

They apparently didn't think I was a freak and we engaged in a refreshing conversation well into the night. Chris and Christina were in Budapest with a film crew from Hollywood. The film crew was here making a vampire flick. Chris was a stuntman for the movie. Christina, his wife, was joining him for the filming as she was heavily pregnant with their baby due to be born this summer.

"Budapest is a perfect location for filming," Chris explained. "Because of its history, there are neighborhoods with architecture from every European period. For this movie, we are doing a lot of filming in the subways. The subways of Budapest are fucking beautiful. They really put New York to shame."

Our conversation continued and I told them I was in Budapest as a governess with a family from Chicago. "But I'm from Alaska," I said.

"Alaska!" They both nodded and seemed pleased. "Alaska is so cool." Chris said. "Hey," he leaned in and softened his voice, "In Alaska, I hear you have pretty good weed."

Beaming, I replied, "The best!"

Chris smiled and looked over to Christina. She raised her eyebrows knowingly and shrugged.

"Hey," Chris said, "Do you want to smoke some weed? I've got a few joints in my room."

Of course, I did. Chris went with Christina back to their room and came back alone. She wanted to rest, what with being heavily pregnant. The two of us left the hotel and found a secluded spot by the river in which to partake of the herb.

When we had secured sufficient privacy, I asked Chris how the hell he found herb in Hungary. I thought it was hard to find weed in Europe outside of Amsterdam. He winked and subtly reminded me that he was in the entertainment industry. Chris' discretion was comforting and spoke to his character.

"So how do you like your job, Boopsie?" Chris asked as he lit one up.

"I mean, it's all right," I affirmed between coughs. The weed was harsh but effective. "I'm getting to see the world, you know, but…" I hesitated to complain, "The ten-year-old is driving me crazy."

"Yeah, kids are hard," he kindly acknowledged.

I realized my faux pas and tried to smooth it over, "But congratulations on becoming a father, man. Your kid is gonna be great."

"Yeah, Christina will be a great mother. College is gonna be expensive though," he added with a lighthearted smile. "Boopsie, don't you think it's kinda fucked up that this family can't take care of their own kids? They had to hire you to look after them."

Chris had expressed the very same sentiment Alice had, and I could finally hear the profound wisdom in the words. Perhaps it was the perspective gained by imbibing the herb or maybe having faced the last few weeks with the Smiths. Chris' words rang of truth. The enormity of my present predicament with the Smith family almost paralyzed me.

Nodding in acknowledgment to Chris' comment, I did not want to dig deeper, so I changed the subject. He told me about the movie he was working on. We discussed politics in America, where we were on 9/11, and the hard times that are sure to come for our nation. Chris was a man of quality, and I enjoyed our conversation immensely. The sentiment was mutual, it seemed. Walking back to the hotel, Chris gave me his email address and his phone number.

"Hey Boopsie, if you ever come out to California, look us up. I could introduce you to some people. If it turns out being a governess is not for you, we can get you a job in Hollywood."

Doctor Gabor

⁓∾∾⁓



I t was our final day in Budapest. Sitting together with the entire Smith family in the morning at a large round table in the hotel's breakfast room, Mrs. Smith informed me she would like for me to meet Mr. Smith's doctor that afternoon. I agreed. And afterward, she said, I should take Emma and Mandy out for dinner and put them to bed. Mr. and Mrs. Smith had a romantic dinner date planned.

I mentioned that I had met some of the American filmmakers whom we had noticed were staying in the hotel. Mr. Smith leaned in with intense interest and asked if I could introduce him to the film crew. I raised my eyebrows and shrugged off his request.


I had the morning to myself, but I needed to be back to the hotel by 3:00 pm to meet the doctor. Reluctantly, due to the fear I might be implicated in a poisoning, I decided to wander about and say my farewells to the great city of Budapest. As I exited the hotel, I glanced guiltily at the hotel clerks, wondering if they had heard of a poisoning in the park.

Stepping into the streets, I noticed all the shops and restaurants were closed. Very few other people were out, and it was eerily quiet. Trekking down to the banks of the Danube, I was treated to a happy surprise. There I learned why the tourist district was empty and where all the people had gone. I discovered a raucous parade! I pushed through the throng of spectators, looking for a good place to view the spectacle. There were very many people walking as participants in the grand parade. Different branches of the military sported their fancy dress as they marched in lock-stepped rows. Floats were designed gayly as animals. Some were covered in flowers. Dignitaries waved from the back of slowly moving convertibles. Folk bands played bagpipes and strange stringed instruments as they sauntered the parade route. Dance troupes decked in traditional Hungarian attire danced around them. In the skies above the crowd, jets from performed stunts and risky maneuvers to the amazement of the crowd.

Following the parade, I weaved in and out of the crowds until I reached its terminus in front of the massive gothic-style Hungarian parliament building. I heard someone speaking good English and I asked them what the parade was for.

"It's State Foundation Day," they told me.

I guessed that it was like the Fourth of July in America. My curiosity and taste for adventure both satisfied, I turned into the city and away from the crowds.

At Vorosmarty Square, I was treated to a mass of stalls selling breads, cakes and pastries. In full confession, I tried one of everything, until I was stuffed and found it painful to move. But, hey, it was my last day in Hungary. It was now or never.

Unfortunately, I was obligated to return to the hotel to meet Mr. Smith's doctor. Walking back was uncomfortable after having gorged on cakes. However, the ambulation served to aid my digestion and I felt better by the time I finally reached the elevator and ascended to the sixth floor.

Mr. Smith greeted me and introduced me to their guest. "Boopsie, please meet Dr. Gabor."

"Hello," I smiled sweetly and hoped I made a good impression.

Doctor Gabor was short and a little pudgy around his waist. His closely cut salt-and-pepper hair and beard were more black than white. I reached out my hand to greet him with a handshake, and I noticed that he blushed. Was that inappropriate? I didn't know the cultural norms as they would apply to the meeting of a doctor and a young woman in a hotel room. We weren't alone. The entire Smith family was gathered there on sofas as witnesses to the exchange. Surely it was not improper to offer my hand.

Small talk ensued and I was mostly a silent observer as Mr. Smith dominated the conversation as usual. When a good opportunity arose, I excused myself, asking the girls to come with me so that we could ready ourselves for dinner. Scootching past the family on the sofas, I was forced by the close quarters to rub up against Doctor Gabor, who sat elevated on the arm of one of the sofas. I felt self-conscious about it. He was reluctant to even shake my hand, then I rubbed my pelvis against his knee. *Oh, Boopsie!* Looking back for the last salutation, I saw Doctor Gabor had an erection in his pants.


The shops and restaurants in the tourist district had opened again. The girls and I chose to eat at a Cuban restaurant called Havana Cafe. It was a hip place with vaulted ceilings, arched doorways, and Castro photos and memorabilia on display. The three of us had already ordered when, glancing out the window, I saw Mr. and Mrs. Smith looking in. They'd seen us too. Mrs. Smith, wearing Scarfy, rolled her eyes and Mr. Smith scowled dramatically.

I gathered they were planning on coming to the Havana Cafe for their date. What was I supposed to do? Take the children to McDonalds? Mr. and Mrs. Smith stared unmoving for a bit. Then she noticeably sighed and led him by the hand into the restaurant. They apparently resigned themselves to joining their girls and I at our table for their romantic dinner date.

"Boopsie, thank you for meeting my doctor today. You made a good impression on him," Mr. Smith said.

"Oh, of course. I hope his work is helping you." I said with trepidation knowing he'd been staying back sick at the hotel for some days.

When Mandy left the table to find the bathroom, Mrs. Smith

said, "Boopsie, maybe now is a good time to tell you that we will be moving to New York."

I was taken aback. Leia and my friends were in Chicago. I'd become comfortable driving there and navigating the Smith's neighborhood. What about Professor K——? I didn't know what to say.

Mr. Smith chimed-in. "I have a doctor in New York too. Dr. Gabor thinks I should be closer to that doctor for the time being."

Our conversation was interrupted when Mandy returned to the table in a huff. She had asked a waiter where the bathroom was. The waiter misunderstood her and thought Mandy had shit her pants. The waiter started speaking in a panic to her in Hungarian and the awkward exchange spiraled into trauma from there.


When the girls were tucked into bed and Mr. and Mrs. Smith were settled in their room, I went out into the city one final time. Knowing I had to be back in time to catch the ride to the airport for our red-eye flight to America, I didn't wander far. At the park I discovered a free concert by the Hungarian Symphony Orchestra. I scanned the audience seated on picnic blankets in the grass, thinking I might see Otto and Roman. I didn't, so I plopped myself down on the grass and enjoyed the concert alone. This beautiful end to my adventure in Budapest only became more beautiful. Fireworks celebrating the Hungarian holiday lit up the night sky above the symphony's stage.

Taking in the grandeur of the moment, I lit a cigarette. Families on blankets beside me gave me ugly looks and shouted at me in Hungarian. They were presumably telling me to stop smoking. I stamped the cigarette out in the grass. To piss them off, I left the butt there as revenge litter and walked away into the night.

# Adieu, Budapest



*AUGUST 21, 2002 (SOMEWHERE OVER THE ATLANTIC)*

All good things must come to an end, and my time in Budapest is no different. I've had the time of my life in Hungary and will remember my adventures here forever. I've had a taste of travel and I want more.

As Professor K—— had said, "A year of travel will teach you more than a lifetime of books." We were only in Hungary for a few weeks and a lot was learned. Not only about another corner of the world, but about myself. Surely I am not the same girl who arrived a few weeks ago wide-eyed with wonder. I've been changed by my time in Budapest. Changed by the perspective I gained. Changed by the people I met. Changed by the joys and the disappointments, the frustrations and the pleasures I experienced aplenty in Hungary. Most evidently, I've been changed by the espresso, egg cream, pastries and tender meats. I have gained at least ten pounds.

Truth be told, it'll be good to have my own bed again. Mandy and I grew close during our travels, but there's only so much a grown woman can take. My attic abode calls to me, promising solitude, comfort, and privacy.

Our hotel arranged for a microbus to take us to the airport for our flight back to the West. Lo and behold, we were nearly out of the tourist sector when Mr. Smith realized he forgot the plane tickets in the hotel. He forgot the tickets. Again! I hoped Mrs. Smith would take charge of the tickets for our trip to Egypt. Or maybe I should volunteer for the responsibility. But no worries, there was not a lot of traffic, and we only lost a little time retrieving them. It had become almost routine to turn back round for the tickets. Perhaps that was why Mrs. Smith insisted on arriving at the airport three hours early.

Our minibus driver was not clued into Mrs. Smith's well-practiced plan. Anticipating the return to the hotel would cause us to be late, or maybe certain it would cause him to be late to his next appointment, he sped, weaved, and swerved dramatically in an attempt to gain time. When we were nearly at the airport, a merging taxi sideswiped our minibus. Mr. Smith flipped out.

Throwing up his arms he hollered, "God damn it!" Looking frantically around the bus he surveyed our condition. "Is everyone okay?" he asked with equal intensity.

Mrs. Smith assured him everyone was fine while the driver jumped out of the bus. We heard our driver hurl heated words at the other taxi driver. Thankfully, the children didn't understand Hungarian. It was, judging by the tone and volume, not a child-friendly exchange.

Miraculously, our luck turned, and we checked in for our flight without any problems. I was buzzing as I reflected on my time abroad. No, I was really buzzing. I felt a vibration and I thought maybe my nervous system was going haywire due to the lack of sleep. Then I thought maybe this was the kundalini experience of the yogis. As one reached enlightenment, their chakras tuned into the resonance of God, one-by-one up the spine until the third-eye opened and one saw God's plan with clarity. The kundalini experience opened a person up to how it all is, the oneness of creation. It was the ultimate yogic experience, and it was happening to me, Boopsie O'Flannigan from small-town Alaska. I was about to transcend Earth. So long, cruel world. See ya, suckers. I psychically braced myself for the abyss.

But alas, dear readers, 'twas not kundalini energy wending up my spine. Nor was lack of sleep playing tricks on my nervous system. I realized as we were standing in line for the baggage check, Johnny Rocket, the giant silver vibrator, had switched-on in my backpack. Oh, fuck! All the blood in my body rushed to my face. I couldn't breathe. Why the fuck did I pack Johnny Rocket in my hand luggage? What was I thinking?

It was my turn to place my backpack in the conveyor belt to be x-rayed. Johnny Rocket kept rocking. I braced myself for the unknown. What should I do? Should I excuse myself and run to the bathroom to turn the damn thing off in privacy? I should stay with the Smith family and not separate? I couldn't possibly take it out and switch it off here in front of everyone. Could I reach into my bag and do it stealthily before it went on the conveyor belt? Not without attracting the attention of security. Drawing a deep breath, it'd be my last until the mortifying situation was resolved, I placed my backpack on the conveyor belt. Unbreathing, I watched as it advanced through the x-ray system.

As expected, the conveyor belt stopped as my bag was directly in the center of the machine. This was going to be bad. I pictured my shameful future:

*Security signals me to step aside. The Smiths are confused, aghast, ashamed. The entirety of cueing passengers and the security staff watch as my vibrating metallic dildo is pulled out of my luggage by a gloved pincer grip. It's a living nightmare. It's surely not illegal to bring a vibrator on a plane, was it? I won't be arrested. I won't be banished from Europe. I will surely be dismissed by the Smiths. Will I have to leave directly upon arrival in Chicago? Where will I go?*

When the conveyor belt restarted and my bag was returned unopened to me, I nearly collapsed. The blood rushed back to my joints and I could breathe again. Either the operating dildo didn't catch the attention of the security screener, or realizing there was a buzzing dildo in my backpack, they were discreet about it. Either way, I was a lucky bitch.

Alice is going to hear about this. It was her brilliant idea for me to bring the damn thing on my adventures. This is the last time I travel with a vibrator. Mark my words.

## AUGUST 22, 2002

It felt incredibly good to wake up in my own bed. Ok, it was technically not my bed. It felt good to wake up in my own country. Yes, faithful readers, we were back in America. Feeling positive I readied myself for the day and descended to the kitchen.

It was back to the grind for your favorite governess. Hotel staff were not there to clean-up after breakfast, and it seemed as though breakfast preparation today included throwing cereal into all corners of the kitchen. Mrs. Smith was in the dining room with the girls. I said good morning. She tasked me with washing the laundry.

"Sure," I said.

"And Boopsie, today you need to drive with Mandy to the kennel where we lodged Tooty and bring the dog home. I'll give you a blank check to pay the kennel fees."

"No problem."

After cleaning the remains of an apparent party in the kitchen, I ascended the stairs, still in a cheerful mood.

Stepping into the parents' suite to gather the family's laundry, I glimpsed Mr. Smith in his underwear. Frankly, I was nonplussed.

Mr. Smith, however, seemed bothered. Exclaiming, "Eek!" He pranced into the ensuite bathroom.

"Good morning, Mr. Smith. I'm getting the dirty laundry." I'd been sophisticated by my time in Europe. Nudity there was normal and natural. Mr. Smith's tighty whities and full bosom didn't faze me in the least.

While the laundry washed, I drove with Mandy to the pet store to pick-up dog food and a new collar. Then we were off to the kennel to retrieve Tooty. Despite their troubled past, Tooty seemed excited to see Mandy. At least, he was excited to be sprung from the kennel. He barked and pranced and wagged his little docked tail. I too was in a cheerful mood. I promised Mandy we would take the dog for a walk as soon as we got home. Despite my lengthy pause from automobile operation, I was okay driving in Chicago. I was only a little stressed and mostly cheerful.

When one load of laundry had been shifted to the dryer and the next begun, Mandy and I took Tooty for a walk through the Smith's neighborhood.

"I don't know about you, Mandy, but I'm really happy to be home," I said to her.

"Me too. I'm excited to start school next week," Mandy replied cheerfully.

"If you want, we can arrange a playdate with your friends. They can come over and swim in the pool. I'm sure your mother will say it's fine."

"Thank you, Boopsie!" It was cute how she lisped the 's' in my name.

I smiled for having pleased her.

Mandy jumped up and down with her hands raised above her head in exaltation. The momentary lapse of hand control allowed Tooty's leash to fall from her hand. I stopped admiring Mandy's show of reverie, as I saw Tooty's escape unfold in slow-motion. Tooty sprinted off down the street. Attempting to stop him, I stepped on the leather leash trailing behind him, but failed. He was running wild and free through the neighborhood. Mandy and I gave chase. We followed Tooty for more than a block when we saw him turn into a long driveway and slip under the fence of a neighbor's backyard.

It was the back of a large white house with two flowering trees planted symmetrically in the spacious front lawn. Following Tooty's path of escape, we walked down the driveway lined with ornamental hedging. It was a dead end. Tooty was definitely in the backyard of this house, he couldn't have gone anywhere else.

"Mandy, let's ring the doorbell. Do you know these neighbors?"

"Yes. I know this house. It's Mr. Farbermann's. He's friends with Daddy. He's a doctor. He has teenager kids. The girl used to babysit me."

"Good. Then he will help us." My optimism faded when no one answered the doorbell. Despite repeated attempts and several minutes of waiting on the front porch of Dr. Farbermann's house, the door remained closed and Tooty remained in the back yard.

Desperate to retrieve Tooty, Mandy and I reconnoitered the perimeter of the property. We identified a spot where Mandy could fit through a gap in the fence. She shimmied through and screamed. The screams of a grown man followed and then a litany of very adult swear words. Dr. Farbermann must've been home after all. Maybe he didn't hear the doorbell because he was in the backyard. But no problem. It was a simple mistake, I surmised.

Unfortunately, the mistake was much more complicated than simple. Dr. Farbermann had been home. He hadn't heard the doorbell ring because he had been in the backyard doing Tai Chi. Naked. In the sanctity of his own backyard, he was doing Tai Chi in the buff. A ten-year-old girl squeezed through the fencing protecting his home and screamed at the display of his naked body as it tranquilly went through the motions of his Tai Chi routine. He was understandably freaking out.

For her part, Mandy thought she would find her little doggy in an empty backyard of a well-known neighbor. Instead, she saw a grown man's naked body. She was freaking out.

I apologized to a now robed-in-silk, but still red-in-the-face, Dr. Farbermann. He curtly handed me Tooty's leash, muttered a few more swear words - something about "breaking and fucking entering" - and stormed back into his house.

Mandy was distraught and I did everything I could to calm her down. "Listen, Mandy. Nudity is natural. It's normal."

She was calming down as I gave her my full attention and reassurance.

Speaking in a soothing tone, I continued, "It's natural. Haven't you ever seen your dad naked? Why, just this morning I saw your dad in his underwear."

Mandy winced. I had said too much.

How was I going to explain this to Mr. and Mrs. Smith? I was not cheerful anymore.

---

I've awoken suddenly in the humid night. Flashes of a dream still linger: Roman said he would drive to see me every weekend. Paul Newman, the salad dressing guy, was sponsoring me and my band of mercenaries to commit murder. I recall a snowy fall from a tower. After the tumble, I had a hard time putting three pairs of socks back on my feet.

Why was I wearing three pairs of socks? Tower dreams are bad omens. Something is amiss.

# Hello, Mandy



**W**elcome to my diary, Mandy. Please, make yourself comfortable and show yourself around my psyche. What can I do to make your intrusion in my private places more enjoyable? Add one more to your ranks, dear readers. Mandy read my diary.

After this morning's workout, I went to the basement and piled all of yesterday's laundry into a basket that I might fold and place each family member's clothing back into their respective drawers. Setting Mandy's t-shirts in her wardrobe, I noticed a piece of paper folded into crisp thirds. It was tucked away in the back of her other shirts and I intuitively knew it was something I was going to want to see. Written in blue ink, the bubbly letters of a preteen girl revealed a great many of the secrets in this house. Hers and mine.

*I actually, finally have a solid judgment on Boopsie. She*

*is a wolf-he-hem-monster in sheep's clothing. She is a drink-ing, smoking, mean person. You can say a person is mean and not mean it, because nobody is always mean, but I can be sure when I speak of Boopsie.*

*I found her diary near Emma's crib and because I was curious, I picked it up. It is normally a terrible thing to do, but I didn't think. I read about myself. She continuously swears, tells how much better Emma is than me, and is a horrid witch. So what if I love dogs? What if I'm even obsessed with dogs? I don't care. The things she says are so mean I can't put much on the page. She says I think I'm the "queen of the world". She says pages more, but nobody can copy a whole diary anyway.*

*But things I am most angry about are - 1. She thinks nobody is better than anybody else, which is supposed to be true, but come on. What if you live in a middle eastern country and you are a woman. You're shut up in a box thing with other women, with a tiny peephole to look out of. You are viciously thrashed with a whip if you even show an ankle and are almost dying from blood wounds.*

*We are better than that government.*

Dear Readers, did I ever write that Mandy thinks she is the 'queen of the world?' I don't think so. I don't remember. Maybe I did. It doesn't matter. But I do care that she read my diary. I hope she learned a lesson. She wrote that she now knows about my true 'drunk nature.' Ha! What a provincial little rag.

I think I have to quit or I will surely be fired. But honestly, I'm not ashamed, nor dreading dismissal. I might relish such a turn of events. My only stress is that I had so many boxes of books sent to the Smith home. If I've left by the time my boxes arrive, I will have the family send them back to my parents' address in Alaska. I've learned many lessons from this unfortunate event. One of which is,

in this line of work, one must always be able to pack up what they
own on their back and leave. Jane Eyre must've been a minimalist
too.

*What to do with you now, my dear diary and friend? Your sanctity has been
shat-upon. Very easily I could toss you into Lake Michigan. Such a poetic fate
for such a poetic object. To cast you away seems a satisfying thing. But first, my
confessor, please be a sympathetic ear to my day.*

After confronting Mandy and admonishing her infringement upon
my privacy, I went alone to the library. I intended to use the internet
to search for a new job. In addition to several job leads, I found a
love letter from Roman.

> *Dear Boopsie,*
>
> *I write to you to tell you what a good time we had with you in Budapest.
> Otto and I have both returned to Germany now. I spoke with Otto yesterday
> and we remembered our night together. If you ever come back to Europe, we
> hope we will see you again. Do you still want to go to Cuba?*
>
> *Sincerely,*
> *Roman*

Attached to the email were three photos. One photo was of
Roman and Otto smiling into the camera from close range. One
was of the three of us seated together on the sofa in his Budapest
apartment. And one photo was the picture the brothers had taken
of my smoking puffin tattoo. Seeing it from that angle, I thought my
tattoo looked great.

*But what to do about my faithful diary? If I should keep it, my time remaining
with the Smith family would be awkward, unbearable, intolerable! If I were to
destroy it, I would be breaking my principles. I know I'm in the right here. Mr.
Smith keeps a diary too, and I would never think of reading it. It's unthinkable!
It's indecent! That little beast Mandy had no right to read this diary.*

Returning home from the library, I met Mrs. Smith on the landing of the stairs as she exited her home office. She handed me a check and said, "I'm firing you.

Oof! Well, I figured.

"Can I please have an explanation," I calmly and evenly asked.

"No. I can't give you an explanation."

"I deserve an explanation," I held my ground and kept my chin up.

She sighed. "My loyalties are torn here. I can't give you an explanation. I'm sorry."

"Well, in a situation like this, all parties should be happy," I conceded with dignity.

"Be out by the weekend," Mrs. Smith concluded.

I took the severance check from her extended hand and climbed to the attic. *What now?*

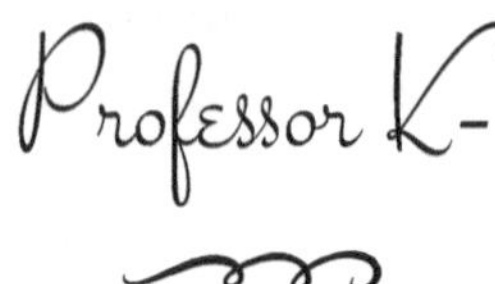

Calling Leia from the tan, corded, push-button phone in the attic seemed the best course of action.

"Hey," Leia answered. "How was Budapest? I'm glad you're back."

"Budapest was fucking amazing. But Leia, I got fired."

"Just now?"

"Yeah. They wouldn't tell me why, but I think it's because the eldest daughter read my diary and…the diary is fucking nasty."

"They wouldn't tell you why?"

"Yeah. Can I come and stay a couple nights with you? I want to get the fuck out of here."

"Yeah. Listen, Boopsie, I got totally kicked out of the artists' collective. They found out I was still in the building, squatting in a little hidey-hole. I'm staying at Evita's place now. But yeah, you can crash here too. It's no problem, I'm sure."

Looking out the attic window onto the driveway of the Smith's house, I saw a postwoman carrying familiar boxes up to the porch. The boxes in which I sent my worldly possessions from Alaska. *What timing!*

"Leia, I've got to go. I'll call you tonight before I come over."

It was Friday afternoon. I had to get those boxes to the post office and mail them back to my mother in Alaska before the damned post office closed for the weekend… in thirty minutes.

I grabbed my purse and headed downstairs. The house was quiet and seemed empty. Mr. and Mrs. Smith must've been napping, or lounging or whatever it is they do with their privileged multi-millionaire afternoons.

The beautiful postmistress was heaving my box of books to the front step of the porch. I ran out to greet her. I was amazed the boxes arrived in time for me to return them before my forced exit from the Smith house. It was a miracle. Seeing all of the possessions I had shipped from Alaska in anticipation for my new life in Chicago, I realized they were but stones weighing me down.

*Let my compassionate readers who may consider this ghastly profession heed these words of wisdom: Take only what you can carry on your back.*

With haste, I hauled the boxes into the trunk of the dilapidated Camry for one last wild ride. I had twenty minutes before the post office closed for the weekend.

Stressed beyond belief, but successful in my quest, I made it to the post office before it closed. Standing at the back of the line in triumph, I surveyed the scene. Some asshole pushed me in line. *Be Zen, Boopsie. Be Zen.* Focusing on my heart, I took a deep breath and calmed myself. It was two minutes before closing.

Making it to the head of the line, the next customer to be served, with only two minutes to spare before the place closed down, I felt lucky. Until some fucking lady cut blatantly in front of me. What made this crap-face so important? Was it the same asshole who pushed me earlier? I couldn't tell these blue-hairs apart. *No problem, Boopsie. Zen, Zen, Zen. Think of Gandhi.*

Everyone in the post office saw I was wronged. If it had come to fisticuffs, the other patrons would have supported me. But did they not respect my passive acceptance? American culture was increasingly aggressive and rude. It had been postulated by many smarter people before me, that for a woman to be successful in the American business sector, she must be extremely aggressive, even overtly masculine. Masculine! Passivism was considered weakness in America. It was as though the Christians had forgotten Christ. Not me. I kept my cool.

Finally at the counter, the postman turned my boxes over skeptically, "This tape won't hold. I can't ship this."

I lost my cool. "Well, I just had it shipped all the way from Alaska, exactly like this. I even reinforced the tape job with some tape I purchased, here, at this very post office on this very day. The tape should be good. Why would you sell me this tape if you won't accept its potential to prepare packages for shipment? I just bought this tape. Here. A few minutes ago."

The postman grumbled, "Maybe someone else would accept it." Then he grumbled some more.

Sighing, I stepped aside to reinforce the reinforced tape affixing my boxes for shipment. I felt a million pounds lifted off my chest when they were finally accepted, out of my possession, out of sight, on their way back to Alaska. I kept my flute with me though, in the case I may need to play in the bus station for dimes. You never know.

Heaving a sigh of relief and inhaling the anxiety of not knowing what the future holds, I plotted my next stop - Professor K——'s house. Zipping up Sheraton Road, I got caught in Friday commuter traffic, which gave me time to slow down and think. I hadn't warned Professor K—— that I was coming. In fact, he was not even apprised of the fact that I was in Chicago. Should I turn around and go straight to Evita's apartment? But I was in distress, and he was the reason I was here, and, well, what had I got to lose?

Unannounced, I found Professor K——'s prairie-style house and rang the bell. Hearing footsteps approach the door, I fantasized about our first beholding of each other in years. Overcome with surprise, he would sweep me up in his arms, and breathlessly exclaim, "Oh, Boopsie, it's you!" We would kiss and melt into each other.

I was speechless when Professor Sanchez opened the door wearing only silk boxer shorts. Professor K——'s voice called from within the house, "Honey, who is it?"

Without a word and now wiser, I pivoted 180 degrees and walked back to the Camry. Professor K—— was not an ascetic as was my worst fear. Professor K—— was homosexual.

Driving back to the Smith's house to pack my few remaining

belongings, I tried my best to make sense of the situation I found myself in. Emotionally overwhelmed, I was unable to cry. Oh, Professor K——. *Unrequited love knoweth my name and utters it repetitively and cruelly.* I was certain that he had loved me. I, somewhat shamefully, hoped his repressed academic temperament punished him every day, longing for me. Wishing our situation was different. Quietly brewing resentment that Professor Sanchez was not me. Clearly, I was quite sensitive. Damn! I knew he still thought fondly of me, perhaps even thought of me as a love. Maybe he would think of me as the one who got away, tossed away by carelessness. More likely this was simply another case of unrequited love.

# Evita

Mr. Smith drove me to the train station so I could ride into the city and off into the sunset. Not a word was exchanged in the short car ride. He didn't know it yet, but I managed to sneak away one more of his pens before my departure from the Smith family home. I planned to use it to write in my diary tonight as I processed the day's humiliations. Only a nod was exchanged as I exited the car and hauled my backpack out of his obnoxious BMW. I took the L train to Evita's apartment on Lawrence Avenue.

Leia greeted me at the door with a big hug. It was nice to see a true friend and I relished her healing embrace. Since Mrs. Smith fired me on the staircase, my world was turned upside down and healing was in order.

Evita had a big, beautiful apartment located on the third floor of a three-story red-brick building that had three units on each floor. It was spacious and lit by big bay windows in the living room overlooking Lawrence Avenue. I was to sleep on the couch in the living room, so I left my backpack on the floor propped up against the side of the couch. Evita shared the apartment with her new roommate, another dominatrix, Ms. Cleo. Leia brought me into the kitchen where everyone was sitting at a retro 1950s diner table.

"Hi, Evita," I said shyly, wondering sensitively if I was putting her out by crashing unexpectedly at her house.

"Hi, Boopsie!" Evita welcomed me with genuine pleasure. She stood up from her red-cushioned chair and opened her arms wide for an embrace. I was relieved and relaxed. Evita's kindness almost made me cry.

Evita was voluptuous and beautiful. Her eyes were lined with thick black eyeliner, but otherwise, she was a natural beauty, as evidenced by the hair under her arms allowed to grow in unabated tufts. Evita was vegetarian and had a tattoo of a bundle of asparagus on her arm. However, she couldn't entirely give up on animal products, as her line of work required copious amounts of leather.

Evita, Leia, and I all went to college together, so I knew Evita was brilliant. She grew up in Virginia, the daughter of a federal agent and a college librarian. She was a gifted pianist and I understood she had a way with the whips.

Evita introduced me to her roommate Cleo. Cleo was tall and thin. Her blunt black bangs framed her angular face, which was adorned with thick-rimmed, black glasses. Evita told me she and Cleo had been touring the country with a collective of sex workers who put on cabaret shows. The aim of the events was to advocate for the decriminalization and destigmatization of sex work.

"It's the oldest profession in the world, no?" I added.

"If sex work were decriminalized, we could control who, when, and where we meet. And we would have recourse to the law when we meet bad men. You see," Evita explained, "criminalizing sex work only serves to make it dangerous for women."

"Maybe that's the point," I quipped. "For all that we have equal rights, our society is still misogynistic."

"Oh, it's true," Evita agreed. "But most men are as damaged by misogyny as we are."

Leia chimed in. "One thing I realized when I was stripping was that men are hurt and vulnerable too."

"The system doesn't work for anyone," Evita concluded.

Ms. Cleo, I learned, had a heroin habit. As Evita waxed

eloquent about her work, Cleo fell asleep sitting at the kitchen table with a lit cigarette in her hands. No one seemed concerned, so I tempered my initial apprehension and intuitive urge to shake her by her shoulders and shout at her to wake up. Instead, I relaxed into our cozy conversation.

The doorbell rang and I met another regular member of the household, Pest. Pest was Evita's house mouse. He did all the cleaning around the house as his preferred method of satisfying his penchant for humiliation. He was an unassuming and relatively young guy. I'd say in his early thirties. He was a small and bearded brunette who reminded a little of Charles Manson with a slightly hunched back.

"Pay no attention to Pest," Evita instructed. "Don't even pay him the kindness of eye contact. He's only fit to clean our filth."

"I feel like I was the pest of the Smith household. I know how buddy feels," I related.

"But he likes it," Evita said, understanding me.

"So, what happened with the Smith's, Boopsie?" Leia asked.

I told Leia and Evita about my misadventures with the Smiths. Maybe Cleo had heard through her drug daze too. I told them about Mandy reading my diary. It helped to talk about it out loud, especially with kind and supportive friends. They laughed and laughed when I told them some of the outlandish disasters that befell Mandy as I did my best to serve as her governess. Laughing with friends helped clear away the shame. Laughing helped bring light to my unfortunate predicament.

"You should mail Mandy the dildo!" Leia said, causing another fit of hilarity around Evita's kitchen table.

Leia continued. "I should call the Smiths and ask for a reference for you, Boopsie. I'll tell them I'm hiring for a nursery school position."

"Let's have Pest call them tomorrow," Evita said with naughty seriousness. "So, what are you going to do now, Boopsie?".

"I don't know. I brought my flute in case I need to play for spare change."

"I saw that when we brought in your bag," Leia said as the corners of her mouth turned up into a sardonic grin.

"Evita, can you get me work as a dominatrix?"

---

I've been on the sofa in the living room for a couple hours, but I can't sleep. Police sirens blare frequently on Lawrence Avenue and traffic continues regularly even into this late hour. Chicago nights always weigh heavily on my heart.

# Pastries and Pies

*AUGUST 25, 2002*

I woke up to Pest puttering around the apartment with a plastic laundry basket under his arm and braced on his hip. I remembered Evita's instructions to not make eye contact with him, so I raised my eyebrows and turned up my nose. Cleo was awake and was at the kitchen table with a massive mug of coffee. Several newspapers were spread out on the table in front of her. She was doing the crossword puzzle of the Tribune in red ink.

"News junkie, eh?"

Cleo offered me a cup of coffee.

"Thanks," I said. "How are you feeling?"

"Yeah, I'm okay. Do you have any plans today?"

"Evita is taking me to the dungeon. She's going to teach me the fine art of busting balls."

Cleo raised an eyebrow. "Very good," she said.

I asked Cleo if she had any advice for me. This was my first time doing anything in this line of work. She went into her bedroom and returned with a book. It was a coffee-table hardback book of photographs of people in varying states of dress in Lycra and leather get-ups. Each model was in a different outfit and likewise, each was in a unique compromising position. "Thanks," I said after she handed the book to me.

Despite its content, it was not pornography. That is to say, it was classy. I turned each page of the book with quizzical studiousness.

What the fuck? Was this really what I wanted to do? Should I be feeling aroused by these photos? Because I didn't. Was it only the men who got aroused by this? Surely the dominatrix thought of destroying men as merely a chore.

"Cleo, do you enjoy being a dominatrix?"

"It's not bad work."

"I know. You make a ton of money. But... do you enjoy it?"

Cleo put her pen down. "Yeah, you know, that's something that's missing from most conversations about sex work. The pleasure involved. We make a ton of money, and we experience a ton of pleasure. It's not a bad gig."


Evita woke up late in the afternoon. We left to go the dungeon a little early so she could show me the ropes.

The door to the dungeon was painted black but was otherwise unremarkable. Lacking signage, it was indistinguishable as a place of business. In the dressing room, Evita let me try on a few of her work outfits. I chose a hot-pink vinyl number. It made me feel sexy and I even felt confident about my curvy thighs. Black high-heeled boots went over black fishnet stockings. The boots laced up in the back and added four inches to my height.

Readers might ask how this Alaskan woman managed to walk in four-inch heels. Gingerly is the answer, gingerly. Admiring myself in the mirror, I was sure I adequately resembled the aesthetic of Cleo's coffee table book. Perhaps Cleo had been right that the sex worker experiences pleasure too.

Evita took me to her first client and introduced me as her apprentice. The client was a Chicago city police officer. He wanted to be anally penetrated. Evita selected a small purple dildo from the array lined up on a shelf by the door of the appointment room. I was glad Evita did the hard work of insertion. Watching was hard enough for me. The cop complained that the dildo was not big enough. Evita instructed me, her apprentice, to select the next largest dildo to try. I continued retrieving ever bigger dildos until the cop screamed, "Uncle!"


"What do you think, Boopsie?" Evita asked between appointments.

"I mean, it was a little gross. But he paid you five hundred dollars."

The next client had a very special request. He asked to be temporarily circumcised. I thought back to my German friends, Otto and Roman. I appreciated foreskin and wonder why Evita's client did not. I wondered how exactly Evita was going to manage to give him what he sought.

Evita showed me a drawer wherein, among more eyebrow-raising items, was a roll of medical tape. The kind that was meant to be used to secure a bandage to awkwardly placed wounds. Evita stood over her client and dramatically pulled out a length of tape. She ordered me to cut it. Like a surgeon, Evita coolly manipulated the man's foreskin back and taped it down. Thereby exposing the tip of his penis to the air for a prolonged period.

"Now stay," Evita ordered her client. She took my hand and, unspeaking, pulled me out of the room. We had a well-deserved coffee break. After coffee and a croissant, we returned to check on her client. The skin on his penis was dry and flaky. *Oh readers, It was so gross!* The client, however, was grinning from ear to ear. As you probably do as well, dear readers, I felt like puking up my pastry.

Evita told me I could do the next client on my own. Feeling unsure, I entered the appointment room alone. A young guy in a baseball hat was sitting nervously in a chair with his elbows resting on his knees. He had a few pink boxes stacked up on the floor beside him. They appeared to be bakery boxes.

"Hello." I tried to sound cold and hard. I hoped it sounded natural. It didn't feel natural.

"Hi," he meekly replied without making eye contact.

"What are we doing today?" I tried to sound in control.

"I need you to kick me in my balls. Hard."

And so it went. I kicked him in the balls. He wanted to be kicked harder. I tried to kick him harder. He knelt down on his knees. I tried kicking him with a running start and hat finally did the trick. He was balled up on the floor writing in pain.

"I got a DUI last night," the guy said sadly. "I need to be punished."

"Oh, I see."

I saw. . . by George, I saw! I saw what he was getting out of it. Was it this way with all Evita's clients? Were they simply trying to feel contrition for their sins? To reclaim a spiritual homeostasis? The cop? Surely he was a sinner. Cops were overwhelmingly dirty. But then I got it! They were only human.

The guy on the floor got up and sat gingerly on the chair. "My name is Steve," he told me.

Steve pointed to the pink boxes. I opened the top one. It was a banana cream pie. Steve wanted me to smash the pies in his face.

Readers, I did so with gusto. I laughed so heartily when I saw his face covered in cream. I did it again with another pie and we both laughed hard and long. I laughed so hard I was crying. Steve was rolling on the floor again, but this time in uncontrollable laughter. Humiliation, it turned out, could be good, healthy fun.

I couldn't wait to tell Alice about this adventure. I thought I should also call my mom, but she must know nothing of my potential new career pursuit.

Back at the apartment I told Leia about my day. "Leia, I don't think this is for me. I'm going to go back to Alaska."

"No! Don't go back to Alaska, Boopsie," Leia pleaded. "Listen. Since 9/11, the economy has slumped and times are bad for everyone, especially for the girls in Vegas. Buses of professionals have come to Chicago from Vegas and taken the local girls' stripping jobs. I can't work in Chicago in this market."

I tilted my head, not sure where this talk was going.

"Come with me to San Francisco. I know a strip club out there where I can probably find work. It's a unionized strip club, and the liberals out there won't mind my fuchsia hair, rhinestone-studded glasses, and facial piercings. We'll do well."

"Okay, Leia," I agreed. "Let's go to San Francisco."

# Westward, Ho



## AUGUST 26, 2002

"Hi, Mom. Yeah, I'm alright. I was fired by the Smiths. No, everything is okay. I know, I know. Being a governess isn't for me. I'm going to San Francisco with my friend Leia. I will be careful. I love you too. Bye."

I respected sex workers, but hoeing was not for me. Leia's plan was as good as any. I had nothing in Chicago to stay for. Leia had grown up in Chicago. However, most of her family was gone. Leia hadn't really ever known her father. Her mother wasn't keen on the orthodox lifestyle imposed upon her, so she absconded with Leia when she was but a baby. I understood her father resides in Israel. Leia's mother was institutionalized, and I had never been privy to many details. I only knew that Leia spent a majority of her youth rotating through foster homes in the Chicagoland area. Though her parents were gone, Leia still had her maternal Grandmother in Chicago. She asked me to join her as she went to the retirement home to bid her grandmother goodbye before we crossed the country bound for California.

To say Leia's relationship with her grandmother was complicated was an understatement. To classify it as a dysfunctional relationship was an over-simplification. A more accurate description of Leia's relationship with her grandmother was 'madcap absurdity'.

The first time Leia took me to meet her grandmother was after we had known each other for a couple months. Her grandfather was still alive then. Leia, her grandfather, and her grandmother were talking loudly, all of them at the same time. Each was trying to speak more loudly than the other, that one might finally be the one to command the attention of the other two. It was our freshman year of college, and at that meeting, Leia's grandparents asked her how college was. Leia said it was terrible. She told her grandparents that there was shit and piss all over the walls of our dormitory. I looked on with disbelief. That was one way to command attention in a conversation.

Now, both of us were college graduates and sadly, her grandfather was dead. Despite the unfortunate decline in number, the tone and volume of the family conversation remained dramatically high. Leia told her grandmother she had to leave the female artists' cooperative because it wasn't kosher. They tried to force her to eat chicken salad sandwiches with mayonnaise and pork chops, otherwise she couldn't be part of the co-op. Of course, Leia, being a good Jew, refused to eat that shit. Thereby, the co-op threw her out on her ass. Her only option now was to go to San Francisco. She'd miss her grandmother and promised to call every Sunday to check-in.

*Readers may recall Leia had a boyfriend, D. Well friends, sometimes life is stranger than fiction. While I was in Budapest, something strange, almost poetic occurred on this side of the Atlantic. You see, Leia read D's diary.*

After being kicked out of the women's cooperative, Leia went to stay with D. One afternoon, alone in his apartment, she couldn't help herself. Curiosity overtook her. She broke his trust and read the man's diary. She was distraught to read that D confessed to an attraction to feminine chicks. He wrote of women with '*shaved pussies*', which was a clear contrast to Leia. Leia had proclaimed that she is "a man who likes a little color on my nails," and who, well… didn't shave her pussy. In her distress, Leia took D's diary and nailed it to the wall in his apartment. Their relationship was over.


Back at Evita's apartment, whilst packing my backpack, I realized I still had the copy of Jane Eyre I checked out in the Smith's neighborhood library using Mrs. Smith's library card. Leia suggested we use the pages to wipe our asses and blow our noses. I suggested her impertinence bordered on sacrilege. Books were to be cherished and respected as a record of human culture and knowledge. However, I was touched by Leia's gesture. She was such a supportive friend I thought as tears welled up in my eyes. No, we wouldn't destroy the book, but we sure as shit weren't going to return it. Mrs. Smith was going to get a fine, and that was fine by me. I knew a measly library fine wouldn't mean much to a multi-millionaire. Nevertheless, I felt some satisfaction knowing I had inconvenienced her, if only a bit.

My backpack was ready, and Leia had packed an old-timey carpet bag. Then, how to get to San Francisco?

"Should we hitchhike?" Leia suggested.

"No, it's dangerous!"

"But we're together, we could protect each other. I'll conceal a steak knife in my combat boots. You can sit in the backseat and if things get hinky, you can use your hairband to strangle a fucker." Leia smiled mischievously.

"These are dangerous times, Leia. You know how the Manson family met?"

We agreed to ride to San Francisco on the bus. There was a Greyhound bus leaving Chicago at 6:50 am. It would take about sixty hours of driving to get there. Accompanied by Leia, the journey had the makings of another great adventure.


We sit at the front of the bus. I like to be able to see out the front windshield to have the driver's perspective. The other passengers on the bus are a little rag tag, but I'm not one to judge. What must they think of Leia and I? Everyone has a story. Life is hard for everyone. Even multi-millionaires don't always get their way, I've learned.

On the bus, I have plenty of time to write in my diary. I'll write down everything I remember about my time with the Smiths. Mayhaps I will publish a book about it someday. Leia writes jokes in a small notebook. She thinks she'll try her hand at stand-up comedy when we get to California. It is a great idea, and I encourage the pursuit. Leia is so funny I am sure she is destined for fame.

---

Whilst driving through the endless and bountiful fields of Nebraska, Leia led the bus in a rendition of Salt n' Pepa's 'Push It'. I accompanied on the flute. The whole bus sang along to the refrain and bounced to the beat in their seats. This was classic Leia, and everyone on the bus would remember the camaraderie and joy of that moment for their entire lives. Leia had a way of making life fun. When we finished the final refrain and the passengers cheered and laughed, something even more unforgettable occurred. The bus hit a hitchhiker.

I saw it happen through the front windshield. He was a tall and thin figure. His black hair was long, past shoulder length. He wore brown corduroy pants and a plaid shirt under a black canvas jacket. All these details are burned into my memory as is the moment the corner of the bus in front of me grazed him. I heard the thud, and turning to watch out the window beside me, I saw him spin around 360 degrees from the force of the blow. Unbelievably, he stayed upright on his feet.

The bus driver did the right thing and brought the bus to a screeching halt. The passengers on the bus stopped their revelries and stared forward wide-eyed when they realized what happened. The hitchhiker, still on his feet, apologized for the fuss. Except for the shock of the thing, he seemed unfazed. He gestured for the bus to move on, turned, and walked off into the sunset.

# Bubbles



*SEPTEMBER 1, 2002*

While we look for jobs and an apartment, Leia and I are staying in a youth hostel for a few days. Walking through the city at night, we notice the sidewalks of San Francisco shimmer as if they've been made with glitter. Maybe the pleasing glint is simply caused by an additive to the cement mix, but no matter, we consider it a good omen.

Leia showed me a flier she found that advertised for two roommates in the Mission District. We used a payphone next to the hostel to call the number listed on the flier. The person advertising the room told us to meet her in the evening and gave us directions to an apartment on 24th street.

The woman who showed us the apartment, Rachel, was immediately sympathetic. Both Leia and I got a nice feeling from her. Rachel was about our age and originally from New Jersey. She was full figured, especially round about the middle. Her kind face was heart shaped. However, because of an overly generous double chin, it took on a perfectly round shape like a large nerf ball. The shape, combined with the features of her face gave the impression she might have had Down Syndrome. She had a tattoo of a peanut on her forearm and wore rhinestone eyeglasses that bore an uncanny likeness to Leia's rhinestone spectacles.

Rachel moved to San Francisco three years prior for a job as a DJ for a small indie radio station. She was looking for two people to share a room with her to cut down on her rent. She was saving up in the case she might need to quit her job. Rachel hated her job now that grunge music was fading.

"This new indie music is crap," she explained.

The one-room apartment she showed us was in the basement of a four-story building located next to a liquor store. In addition to Rachel's single bed, a simple wooden bunk bed furnished the room. There were also two dressers but not much else of note. The basement room didn't have a kitchen or even windows. I couldn't help but wonder if it was zoned for human habitation. But the price was right, and Rachel seemed cool. We were tempted to take it.

"How is this neighborhood?" I inquired. "I noticed there's a shady-looking liquor store next door."

"Umm, It's okay. Like, yeah, you noticed it's not a gated community." Rachel chuckled. "But I have a security system. Don't worry."

Out of the top drawer of the dresser closest to the single bed, Rachel pulled out a three-striped gym sock within which was an object hanging awkwardly, distorting the tube shape of the sock. Rachel's 'security system,' it turned out, was a hammer in a sock. With an impish smile, she told us to stand back as she started hurling the sock with a hammer around in circles at her side. As the speed increased, she whipped it up over her head and round and round in ellipses like helicopter blades. It was, to be sure, an intimidating sight. It was viscerally clear that the hammer-sock could do real damage. Leia and I agreed to be Rachel's new roommates.


Leia and I will share the bunk bed. I get the top bunk because Leia has ADHD, which causes her to generally stay awake all night. That, coupled with her artist's mania, is a double whammy. If Leia were to be in the top bunk, there would be constant squeaking of the bed as she tosses, turns, gets up, comes down, goes back up…

———

## SEPTEMBER 7, 2002

Unfortunately, Leia couldn't find work as a stripper. And well, what was I supposed to do with a degree in literature? After several days of pounding the pavement, we both managed to land jobs working at Bubbles, a laundromat a few miles down 24th street from our new apartment.

"Mazel tov! Let's go out to celebrate!" Rachel shouted with genuine glee when we told her we found work.

She took us to a drag show in the Mission neighborhood. The establishment wherein the drag show was hosted served as a diner in the mornings, slinging-up typical American and Mexican breakfast fare. At night, tables in the foyer of the cafe were stored in the back and metal folding chairs were placed in rows for a small audience. The cashiers' stand was used as an MC podium. The performers sashayed between rows of dining booths to stand in front of the audience. It was real underground shit.

We had fun and we were treated kindly by the queens. Leia got up and danced outlandishly with the performers at the end of the show. Everyone applauded, even the performers enthusiastically admired her indisputable stage presence.

# Authenticity

NOV. 14, 2002

Thusly passed our first months in San Francisco - working the second shift at the laundromat and frequenting the drag show in the evenings. The girls at the drag shows became our friends. Leia worked on her stand-up routine and it was becoming well-refined.

Working at the laundromat wasn't so bad. When the manager finally trusted us enough to leave us unsupervised, Leia juggled a second gig in the back office taking calls for a phone-sex line. While Leia was engaged in her side business, I kept order in the front of the shop with the customers. I was friendly but no nonsense in my role as the proprietor of the laundromat. Are you attempting to use arcade coins to buy boxes of soap from the dispenser? Hell no! Do you need help folding your fitted sheet? No problem. You're a dime short? I got ya. Whoops, you're about to wash a wool sweater in hot water! Better not.

We settled into a peaceful pace of life, and it was good. Rachel, Leia, and I kept each other company and supported each other emotionally. With the hammer-sock ever near, we felt secure. All was alright with the world.

This evening Rachel didn't meet us at the drag show. We caught up with her back at the apartment. She was sullen and we could see from the redness on her soft, round face she had been crying. She explained she had an argument with her boss at the radio station. He had wanted her to pursue an interview with Hootie & the Blowfish.

"Can you fucking believe it?" We could still hear the hurt she carried from that insult in her voice. "Hootie & the fucking Blowfish! Well, I told him, hell no to that. He insisted I could do the interview, or I could quit. So, girls….I quit."

Who could blame her? Leia and I didn't try to talk Rachel out of her decision, we saw it was the right thing to do if not the only option whereby she might retain her dignity. Instead, we formulated a plan to cheer her up. We'd go out to a bar and drown her sorrows.

Being a special occasion, we eschewed our usual dive bars, splurging instead for a fancy cocktail bar with fancy decor, mood lighting, and plush pillowed benches. Leia called a few of our friends from the drag show and invited them to join us to help cheer up Rachel.

Fresh from a show, the girls arrived at the cocktail bar dressed in full regalia. Sweet Ms. Darcy came in a 1950's house dress, bouffant hair, and pink stilettos.

Darcy leaned in with coy concern. In a soft southern drawl, she addressed Rachel. "So, honey, tell me what's going on."

"I can't do this shit anymore. Music has gone to corporate hell. It's not for me. I can't do it," Rachel explained.

Connie sat beside me in a gold-sequined cocktail dress and massive hoop earrings. In her deep voice she validated Rachel. "I hear you. You've got to do what you've got to do," she said with authority. "I want you to live your truth with authenticity. You have to be who you are and if you aren't down with giving Hootie no platform, well, that's authentic."

"And a public service," Leia added.

"Excuse me," I interjected with hesitation. "Connie, you're a man dressed up as a woman. Isn't that inauthentic?"

"Oh, here we go," Connie pursed her lips and stared sternly into my eyes.

"I am living more authentically than most," she asserted. "Who I authentically am is a man who feels good in a dress and heels. Do you think it's easy? Hell no!"

Darcy added, "Everyday, all across the country, people like us are ridiculed, beaten, and murdered for living our authentic selves. But those of us strong enough, we dare to be ourselves."

What they said made good sense. What person would purposefully don a dress and clutch a handbag knowing they'd get their ass beaten on the regular? They must be facing the risk because there is no other choice. They had to follow their hearts to be their true authentic self.

Connie tilted her head, "What about you, Boopsie? Who is the authentic Boopsie O'Flannigan? Do you think you are authentic?"

Eyes widened at my dressing down. I was silent. I wasn't sure how to answer. Who was I? I was raised with no pretensions. In Alaska, survival was the name of the game. There was no room for airs, pretension, or inauthenticity. I supposed I was living an authentic life, but when asked to put who I was to words, I had to think how to formulate an answer.

"How the fuck else would I be?" I finally replied.

Connie smirked, seemingly satisfied with my answer. Then rolling her eyes at my stiff countenance, she picked-up a velvet pillow bedecking the bench beside her and smacked me playfully with it.

Leia grinned impishly and smacked me with another pillow. She then walloped Connie with it. Connie was phased but returned the assault with a two-handed uppercut. Soon all five of us were buffeting pillows at one another, shrieking in delighted abandon. Seeing our antics, the game passed infectiously through the bar. The entire establishment erupted into a full-blown pillow fight. The pillow fight wasn't as is usually portrayed in movies and cartoons. Feathers didn't spill out from the pillows and drift chaotically through the air. Instead, wigs, eyelashes, martini glasses, and press-on nails flew around the bar.

# The Stars Align

DECEMBER 1, 2002

Within a week, Rachel went back to New Jersey where her parents were executives at a textbook publishing company. They fixed her up with a nice white-collar job in their corporate headquarters, we heard.

Thankfully, with the extra income Leia was bringing in through her phone sex gig, we were able to cover Rachel's portion of the rent. Leia took over Rachel's single bed. I had the bunk bed to myself.

During lulls at the laundromat, daydreams about more meaningful work were starting to creep into my consciousness. I mean, don't get me wrong, I was content with the life Leia and I had made for ourselves in San Francisco. It's only that from time to time, I thought about my adventures in Budapest. I thought about how stimulating it was, and how alive I felt while I was traveling.

Yesterday, Connie came by the laundromat. She asked if Leia would consider working at the drag shows. They needed someone to MC and Leia was perfect for the position. They loved her there. Working the drag show would give Leia an opportunity to practice her stand-up comedy set to a live audience, not only to the guys on the phone-sex line. Toiling at Bubbles and moonlighting at the drag show, Leia could manage to pay the rent on her own. I made the big decision to leave San Francisco and try my fate elsewhere.

I decided to go to Hollywood to find Chris, the stuntman I met in Budapest. Mayhap he and his beautiful wife Christina needed a nanny.


From my adventures with Professor K——, I learned an important lesson about calling before showing up on someone's doorstep. Readers, it's good to learn from other people's mistakes. You too, are welcome to the wisdom I have learned the hard way.

At the bus station in San Francisco, I called Chris before purchasing a ticket for a bus to Los Angeles.

"Hey! Boopsie! It's great to hear from you. Yeah, c'mon over, we'll put some beers in the fridge. I can't wait for you to meet our little guy."

# Book Club Questions

1. Do you think Boopsie is a sympathetic character? Why or why not?

2. Other than becoming comfortable with nudity, how does Boopsie's character grow over the course of the story?

3. How does the setting of the story contribute to it's telling? Would the story be different if it were set in contemporary times?

4. The author, Ludo has said the major themes of the book are class and friendship. What other universal themes can you identify in the story?

# Disclaimer

*This is a work of fiction. Any names or characters, events, or incidents, are the products of the author's imagination. Any resemblance to actual persons, living or dead, or actual events is purely coincidental.*